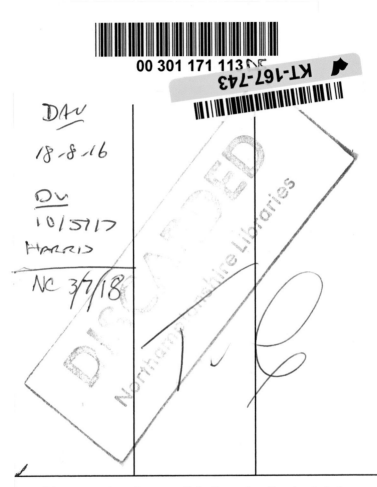
Please return/renew this item by the last date
shown. Books may also be renewed by
telephoning, writing to or calling in at any of
our libraries or on the internet.

Cold, Hard Cash

It seemed the only way to get out of Red Rock Penitentiary was to die and be shipped out as a corpse.

So when Dave Jarrett had a chance to feign his death and be shipped out in a coffin, he took it. But old enemies – and new ones – were waiting. They all wanted him to lead them to $70,000. That was when the brutal chain-gang he had left behind began to look better than dodging bullets at every step.

Cold, Hard Cash

Jake Douglas

A Black Horse Western

ROBERT HALE · LONDON

© Jake Douglas 2011
First published in Great Britain 2011

ISBN 978-0-7090-9299-5

Robert Hale Limited
Clerkenwell House
Clerkenwell Green
London EC1R 0HT

www.halebooks.com

√ITAROS

Typeset by
Derek Doyle & Associates, Shaw Heath
Printed and bound in Great Britain by
CPI Antony Rowe, Chippenham and Eastbourne

CHAPTER 1

'OR DIE TRYING'

This time it was one hell of a beating, the worst so far. Dave Jarrett had lost count of the number of times Corliss had put him in the penitentiary's infirmary. But this was *it*: he'd been here long enough, taken enough hammering from the brutal guard's big fists and been unable to do anything about it. Except suffer.

No longer: this time would be the last – *the final*. He'd escape somehow, or die trying. And he meant that last part: death would be preferable to this, though he sure as hell would like to take Corliss with him.

Don't be greedy! Escape, then think about squaring things. Or don't escape and die trying; it would be all over, one way or another. . . .

He had served four of the seven years allotted to him by sour-faced Judge Nichols, four years of endless brutality, with the fifth about to begin in a couple of weeks.

So that would be the target: get out before the fifth year dawned, or see it from six feet under in an unmarked grave on the hillside west of the administration block.

Decision made!

Only four men had ever escaped from this hell-hole. Three of them had been recaptured, two before they even reached the river, the third in some whorehouse in Cheyenne, drunk as ten Indians with a barrel of moonshine.

The fourth, a man named Pinney, had never been seen or heard of again, though it was recorded that he had drowned while attempting to cross the river in full spate.

He would have been desperate enough to have tried the crossing, anyway; with a posse within rifle shot, what did he have to lose. . . ?

That was how Jarrett saw his own situation: no choice. If he recovered and was returned to the chain gang or the rockpile, Corliss would kill him eventually, *and* there would be no kick-back. It would appear in the paperwork as an accident; any convict working the rockpile was at constant risk of being crushed by falling boulders, or of being too slow to get under cover when a new wall was being dynamited, falling on sharp tools; so many dangers, all potentially lethal, and handy explanations for the guards in charge.

The prison doctor, Asa Langdon, was a gruff, taciturn man heading into his early sixties. He was competent, far above the usual level of medicos hired by the prison system, but he seemed to be ailing with some illness that he was unable to cure. It made him surly and generally antisocial, left him with a gruffness that kept the patients quiet while he worked on them. Which may have been his intention all along.

That was why Dave Jarrett was surprised when, bandaging the prisoner's bruised ribs with a firmness that had Dave gasping, Langdon said: 'You need good support here. A cast would be better but we're out of plaster right now.'

Jarrett must have shown his surprise, widening his blackened, purple-bruised eyes. He blinked when the seamed, gaunt face of the doctor moved in what could only have been a brief smile.

'You're my best customer. I figure you are entitled to a friendly comment or two.'

Jarrett nodded slowly, his neck stiff and throbbing. 'Thanks, Doc,' he rasped. 'Didn't know you cared.'

Working, head bent over Jarrett's battered body, Doc Langdon said, 'I know the so-called code among prisoners: "Keep thy mouth shut or lose thy teeth", or something like that, but could I ask: just what in blazes did you ever do to Guard Number 12, Lacy Corliss, to earn all these beatings . . . and I have to tell you they are getting worse.'

'Or mebbe he's softening me up more, Doc. I never "earned" them beatings. Just – Corliss bein' generous.'

Langdon nodded soberly. 'But there must be some reason. You are here, in my care, three times more often than any of the other prisoners.'

Jarrett remained silent and when the doctor transferred his attention to a gash along Jarrett's jaw, the prisoner said quietly, succinctly,

'I pissed in his parade boots.'

Langdon looked sharply into the battered and lopsided face. After a moment he smiled.

'Well, I'll be damned! Of course, you're referring to the Independence Day parade, where several of the guards were to be presented with long service medals which came with a hefty bonus, I believe, and, of course, Corliss couldn't appear without his best boots to complete his uniform. In front of the governor of prisons, too, so he missed out. . . . It seems he either didn't have a spare pair of boots or . . . couldn't find them.'

Jarrett, deadpan, nodded. 'If he'd looked down the latrine hole, he might've spotted 'em.'

'And how did he learn it was you who – er – had a weak bladder?'

Jarrett smiled then but it cost him pain as swollen muscles moved. He grunted. 'Nicely put, Doc. Aw, there's always someone looking for some way to get on the good side of the guards.'

Langdon nodded slowly. 'Have I – er – tended that someone – recently – here?'

Jarrett gave him a steady stare, shook his head once. 'Wouldn't think so, Doc. Believe he was pronounced dead right where he had his accident; boulder rolled on him. Happened right below where I was workin'. Saw the whole thing.'

Langdon said nothing, but suddenly stepped back, his hands grabbing at his midriff. His old body bent over sharply. He gasped raggedly, now steadying himself with one hand against the bedhead.

'Judas, Doc! You all right?'

Langdon shook his head slowly and Jarrett forgot his own pain for a moment, seeing how sallow and grey the medic looked. 'You – you better sit down, Doc. Will I ring the bell?'

He gestured to the small bell on the bedside table but Langdon shook his head, groped along the bed and sat down on the edge by Jarrett's feet. His head hung and his body heaved as he fought for breath. Jarrett didn't like the sound of it and then the doctor suddenly lunged for the sick pail and vomited violently, down on his knees now. . . .

It was some time before he stopped and, looking like death, clawed his way up and hitched his skinny buttocks on to the edge of the bed again.

'My – my pardon, Mr Jarrett . . .'

'Judas wept. You scared hell outta me, Doc.' Jarrett stopped, fumbled for words. 'I – mean you don't often see a sawbones – sick, like that.'

The medic lifted a hand, dismissing the words. Then the door slammed back and a big man filled the doorway, glanced around and stomped up to the bed. He wore the drab grey prison-guard uniform, the number '12' in metal numerals above his shirt pocket. His face was rugged, closely shaved, the skin gleaming a little. The mouth was wide and thin, had a merciless look to it that matched a similar one in the agate eyes, one of which had a slight squint. Hair protruding from under the uniform cap was brown and curly.

Lacy Corliss glared at Jarrett and the prisoner couldn't help his hands knotting the sheets under that brutal stare. 'When'll I get him back, Doc?'

Langdon swallowed, trying to get enough breath to speak.

'Well, come on! *When. . . ?*'

'A . . . about a week.'

The guard snorted. 'You can do better'n that!' He leaned down and held four gnarled fingers in front of the doctor's face. 'Count 'em, Doc: one, two, three four. Four days. That's when I want him back on the pile.' His thin lips rippled in a brief twist of a smile, his bleak eyes training on Jarrett's taut face. 'Got a new sledge I want to test. Heavier by quite a few pounds. You're elected for the trial, Jarret. Hope you feel honored at the privilege.'

Jarrett couldn't even explain how he felt. *Terrified* might work. Never in his whole life had he known so much fear and apprehension as in these past six months, when he had been foolish enough to fill Corliss's boots with his urine.

He had lived a hard life; rugged was a better word, and he had dodged lead from both sides of the law, from Yankee and even his own Rebel troops; he had ridden through stampedes and storms that would blow the hair out of a man's scalp as it hurled his body half a mile out of the saddle. He had felt cold steel slicing his flesh, had near-choked on gunsmoke, his Colt burning his hand. *Hell!*

He felt as much sick shame at harbouring this fear as he did the fear itself. The prison system, the one the public never got to read about: Rule 1: reduce the population within the penitentiary walls to the common denominator, which was cringing, belly-knotting servility. Rule 2, through 10: Keep on making sure the prisoners obey Rule 1. Well, it had taken almost four years for Jarrett to even show a crack, the beginning of breaking, he knew, helplessly, but these constant hammerings with boots, fists, and whatever tool came within reach of Corliss's big hands were bending him, and this worried him even more than the pain he now knew to expect. He was ready to crack!

Corliss laughed shortly as he watched Jarrett's face. He leaned down towards him. 'Come on, Jarrett! You're the big tough outlaw, ain't you? Or were! Whatever you are now, make the most of it – savvy? 'Cause you may not be comin' here again – except for one of Doc's death certificates.' He stood chuckling, hitched at his heavy belt with its manacles and hardwood billy and six-gun, shifted his gaze to the sagging medic on the end of the bed.

'You don't look too good, Langdon. You oughta see a doctor!' Laughing, he swaggered to the door, paused before closing it. 'Remember – four days!'

When the door closed, Langdon wiped his mouth on a kerchief and looked at Jarrett's skull-like features. 'I'm afraid that man intends to kill you, Mr Jarrett.'

Dave Jarrett nodded once, staring at the door. 'And there'll be no kickbacks, not the way the warden runs

11

this hell-hole. I'll be just one more nameless mound in the graveyard.'

After a few moments, when he had enough breath, Langdon wheezed,

'Unless you could – escape.'

Jarrett smiled wryly. 'I would if I could find a way out, Doc, or die trying.'

'Ye-es. That does seem like the only option.'

CHAPTER 2

THE CADAVER TRAIL

Jarret gasped for breath, felt his chest fighting the constriction of the bandage Doc Langdon was wrapping very tightly around his chest. He had thought the earlier one had been tight, but this was like a horse standing on him.

'Can't – breathe. . . .'

Langdon, greyish-yellow, winked. 'Sure you can. Through your nose. Slow and easy. Your lungs can expand almost normally, but the bandage compresses the ribcage so it doesn't show movement. Breathe quietly and anyone bothering to check will think you're truly dead, but it's only a simulation. Now try to relax.'

'You – you've done this before. . . ?'

Langdon nodded. 'Oh, yes.' He lowered his voice,

gasping out his words, sweat beading his brow. 'We have what we call "the cadaver trail" – from here to some colleagues of mine at Denver Hospital. All strictly illegal, of course, but medicine has to know more about the human body. The law won't allow us to dissect corpses, and it turns a blind eye most times, but there are do-gooders who would accuse us of necromancy, or sorcery and such, and then, of course, there is always the Church. But already our little group has done a lot of work on the circulation of the blood and the way the heart pumps it around the body; we're beginning to understand it much better, also the function of the kidneys – but you don't need to know all that.'

'You – sure. . . ?'

The medic chuckled, went into a fit of coughing, dabbed at his lips with a balled kerchief. 'Don't worry. You won't accidentally go under the knife. We have a small network of – er – enlightened folk, not all male, I might add. They have been informed that you will be coming.'

'I – hope – so! This is the fourth day Corliss mentioned.'

'Don't breathe so fast, man! Easy now – eas-eee. You'll be out of here by the end of this day. We have plenty of "friends": our carpenter who makes the casket, and the shipping clerk in the Riverton depot, the guard in the caboose of the train that'll carry you out of here; their motives may be mercenary but we've been wise enough to make the pay more than adequate and they'll see you get down the line to where it's safe for you to be released.'

'Air! How'm I – gonna get – air!'

Langdon sighed, sat down. 'The casket lid – you'll notice the plain pine edging comes down about two inches all the way around? It need only be *one* inch – there are small chocks of wood in six to eight places that will keep the lid from resting on the casket's main edge in an airtight seal, though that extra inch on the flange will give the appearance of it doing just that. In fact, it'll be raised an inch all the way round, and the free space between each chock, unseen by anyone, will allow plenty of air into the casket.'

Jarrett was feeling mighty strange, maybe from the preliminary medicine the doctor had given him to help him relax, or just plain fear of the unknown. His heart was pounding, his mouth dust-dry. 'Doc, I – I sure appreciate this, but you'll be in a helluva lotta trouble if they . . .'

Langdon, sober now, leaned across the narrow bed. 'You saw me throw up a few days ago. It happens up to a dozen times a day recently.'

'Goddlemighty!'

Langdon raised a bony, shaking hand. 'I've known for some time now that I have a cancer – deep-seated, in either my liver or the pancreas. Nothing can be done, except to wait for it to kill me. So I have nothing to fear from what you called "trouble". Oh, the warden won't be happy to learn that you've "died". I have a signed death certificate all ready, but whatever fuss he makes will be minor compared to what awaits me.' He touched his own midriff, lightly.

15

Jarrett simply stared, hardly noticing that he wasn't straining so much to breathe now he was getting into a workable rhythm.

'It's painful, Mr Jarrett, very, very painful. I'm not heroic. When the pain reaches a certain level, I will simply drink a full cup of very strong laudanum, and drift away into a delrium, until, finally, all life functions will cease and I will be on my way to wherever the Good Lord decides I should go.'

Jarrett stared a moment longer, gasped: 'Wish my hand was free so – I could – shake your's, Doc.'

'This is an inhuman place, Mr Jarrett, run by inhumane people. I believe I can judge a man pretty well, and I have judged you as being a man worth saving.'

Jarrett smiled crookedly, despite his almost overwhelming apprehension. 'An outlaw? A bank robber?'

'You were only captured because you took the time during your getaway from that last hold-up to stop at a doctor's house and send him to the bank where a pregnant woman's time had been accelerated by the terror of the robbery. She was starting to give birth – a *breech* birth, as it happened. She would have died if you hadn't sent that doctor along. I've often wondered why you did it.'

Jarrett took his time answering. 'A few years before, my sister had a breech birth. She died, though the baby lived. I kind of recognized the symptoms in that woman – or thought I did.'

'And here you are because of that good deed. Well, you are about to be repaid, Mr Jarrett. I wish you well.'

'Doc, I—'

'Hush now. Rex, would you get ready to set the lid in place after we lift Mr Jarrett into the casket?' He spoke to a silent, bearded man in coveralls who stood in the shadows, leaning against the infirmary wall. Jarrett knew he was the prison carpenter – and apparently a member of Dr Langdon's "group".

'Wait, Doc!'

'Don't worry, Mr Jarrett. When they remove the lid my accomplice will be there. He'll have a drug to counteract the morphine and its dispersant that I'm about to give you. I thought of using that new drug, heroin, but we don't yet know enough about it, except it is a marvellous pain-killer – though it caused many problems when it was first used in the latter years of the War. Men craved its euphoric qualities. Tragically, some became addicted. But morphine will hold you in a kind of suspended animation until you reach your destination. If it will reassure you, I have done some very complicated and . . . delicate calculations, according to your age, weight and general physical condition. *And* mental condition, I might add. I am confident you will have all the outward appearance of a true cadaver, until my colleague injects the counter-agent. Please have faith in me, Mr Jarrett.'

Breathlessly, Dave Jarrett said, 'Whatever happens, Doc – my – thanks, an' – and—'

Jarrett jumped, squirmed, gritting his teeth as he felt a hypodermic needle puncture his upper left arm. *No going back now!* He thought his lungs would burst. Then there was a rather pleasant sensation of 'drifting', both mentally and physically. A strange mist began to swirl through his brain and he felt as if he was tumbling from a great height, an enormous roaring in his head until he was sure his skull would shatter. . . .

Then, suddenly, there was nothing but endless blackness, as dark as the heavens without stars.

Or as black and silent as the grave.

Rex was putting in the fifth screw of the pine casket's lid when Corliss came into the workshop with its floor covered in curled wood-shavings and sawdust.

'Get that lid off!' the guard blurted and Rex looked up sharply, shifted his gaze from the guard's angry face to Doctor Langdon as the medic came in slowly, breathing hard.

'Doc. . . ?'

'Never mind him!' snapped Corliss. 'Take that lid off.'

Langdon nodded, still fighting for breath. Rex shrugged and removed the screws, lifted the lid and was careful to keep its underside turned towards himself so that Corliss did not see the series of pine chocks that would keep the lid raised enough to enable Jarrett to breathe.

Corliss stepped up to the casket, glared down at Jarrett's still body in the coarse cloth of the prison-provided shroud, the bruising and cuts standing out clearly against the greyish tones of the flesh, the chest immobile. He reached in and turned back one eyelid.

A black, enlarged pupil stared back at him, lifelessly. The doctor reached in and pushed his hand aside.

'For God's sake! You showed him no respect or

mercy when he was alive. Have the decency to show him some regard now that you've killed him.'

Corliss glared at Langdon. 'Your death certificate says he just "suddenly" died! How the hell? He was all right when I seen him a few hours earlier.'

The medic shook his head slowly. 'No, he was not, Corliss. I thought he was dying then but, of course, did not want to alarm him and set back his recovery by saying so. Your – whatever it was that caused his injuries—'

'An accident, Doc, I told you! He fell off a ledge on to a pile of half-broke rocks.'

'Mmmm. Could account for his injuries, but whatever caused them, broken ribs pierced one lung, and one, maybe both kidneys had been crushed. Look, Corliss, it's all in the death certificate I've given the warden. I suggest you ask him to show it to you and then perhaps you will be satisfied. Will you ask him yourself? Or would you like me to chaperone you and I'll make the request?'

Corliss's razor slash of a mouth almost disappeared as he clamped his lips together. His eyes blazed.

'I – don't think we'll bother the warden, Langdon. I mean, if he's happy with the certificate, I s'pose I've got to accept it.'

'I wouldn't say he's exactly "happy", Corliss. Far from it. Perhaps there are too many such certificates with men in your division dying from accidents that seem to me could have been avoided with a little more care on the part of the supervising guard.'

Corliss's nostrils flared. 'All right. The bastard's

dead and that's an end to it! I'm just sorry he didn't live a little longer so I could. . . .'

He broke off, seeing the medic and the carpenter staring at him, realizing he was saying too much. Then, a sudden thought: 'Hey! How come this "kin" of his made their claim so quick?'

'His niece? Oh, it's been a long-standing request, arranged by Jarrett himself. If he did die, by whatever means, he wanted his body to be shipped out to her for burial.'

'An' where would that be?'

With a sly smile, Langdon, gritting his teeth against terrible pain in his midriff, said, 'The warden has details, but they're confidential. Why would you want to know, anyway?'

Corliss glared. 'I'd've enjoyed pissin' on his grave, that's why! Aah, to hell with it! I gotta get back to my work gang.'

Corliss stormed out and Rex and Langdon exchanged glances, both releasing breaths they hadn't been aware of holding.

'Thought that one was gonna blow up in our faces, Doc.'

'Send Jarrett down to the rail depot as soon as you can, Rex. I – I'll feel much better once he enters our pipeline.' He smiled crookedly. 'But in Jarrett's case I prefer to think of it as a *life*line. Rather an appropriate name, for shipping a "dead" man away from this hell-hole, eh?'

Rex nodded, replaced the lid and began screwing it on again.

Jarrett hadn't made a sound, nor a movement of any kind.

To all intents and purposes, he was a dead man, ready to begin his final journey.

Even the necessary prison paperwork said so.

And no one could argue with that.

CHAPTER 3

A FREE MAN?

The bronc-buster called Ben Dodge lifted the front of his hat and used a crumpled kerchief to wipe away the sweat. He was breathing hard and his buttocks ached from that last bronc, a damn big buckskin, a seventeen-hander, and with the temperament of a gut-shot grizzly.

Still, there was some satisfaction now, his sore buttocks hanging over the top corral rail, spine feeling bruised, watching the buckskin snort and paw the ground, its breathing like a booming drum as it decided whether it had had enough, or was aiming to go another few rounds with this stubborn damn horse-breaker.

A middle-aged man in checked shirt and battered curl-brim hat offered him a cheroot, even snapped a vesta on his thumbnail for Dodge to lean down and fire up.

'You've earned that, Ben, and there'll be a slug or two of bourbon before supper if you're so inclined.'

Still breathless and with every muscle throbbing, Ben Dodge nodded curtly.'I am so inclined, Mr Larrabee.'

'You bust broncs for the army?'

Dodge's grey-blue eyes might have sharpened a little at the question, but he nodded again. 'Sort of a pastime, wasn't really my chore. Just liked bein' able to break in my own mount, feel confident then if we had to ride into trouble.'

Chet Larrabee pursed his lips. 'You wonderin' how I knew you'd been in the army?'

'Guess not.' Dodge gestured to his bedroll and the neck of an old army jacket showing amongst the folds. 'Got sloppy, didn't tuck it in proper.'

'Uh-huh. Just that you never mentioned it when I hired you to bust that damn hell-bronc.'

'Never thought I needed to. You told me to bust a stallion your crew'd just brought in, figuring I could give you all some entertainment when I got shot sky-high over the corral rails, but I got him halfway bust before I lost the saddle. Seemed to satisfy you when I climbed back up.'

Larrabee squinted. 'Kinda touchy, though, ain't you?'

'You ask kinda touchy questions.'

'Uh-huh. Leave it there. You finished with that buckskin?'

'I guess. But you'd be better off gelding him. He's got a mighty lot of spirit swirling around in there. Just look at that eye he keeps rolling in my direction.'

'Hell, yeah! You wanta geld him?'

Dodge laughed briefly, pulled at his frontier moustache and drew on the cheroot. 'Not me. I'll ride 'em, but I won't stop 'em doin' their riding.'

Larrabee chuckled. 'OK. You wanna job with me, you got it.'

Dodge looked at him steadily. 'Where you driving your herd?'

'North, to railhead.'

'Where north?'

Larrabee's watery eyes, raw from staring at endless horizons for twenty years on the cattle trails, narrowed slightly. 'You got a preference?'

'Not exactly. Just a place or two I'd rather not go.'

'Uh-huh. I can savvy that. Well, this lot's bound for Red Rock.'

Dodge tried to keep his voice level but he watched closely and saw that Larrabee had detected the small amount of tension that crept into his reply. 'They got a railhead there now?' When Larrabee remained silent, he added, 'Last time I was there it was just somewhere to pass through, quickly, once you saw them penitentiary walls.'

'Railroad threw a spur track out from Greeley, hoping to pick up army business from Fort Collins, I guess.'

'That'd make sense. Worth their gamble?'

'Reckon so. You happy with that as a destination?'

Dodge looked at him squarely. 'I think I – ah, I've been here too long, I reckon. Like to move about, so you pay me for bustin' in the buckskin, and I guess I'll drift.'

'Sorry to lose a man of your talents. Could make you a good deal. Feller I know up there keeps a lot of mustangs he brings down from the Collarbones; could offer you a bonus for every one you break for the remuda.'

Dodge looked interested but firmly shook his head. 'Like to work for you, Mr Larrabee, but I – I'm one of the restless breed and driftin' the other way.'

'On a timetable? An' I might add, you don't look the type to work by the clock.'

'Clock in this case is workin' for the other feller – I'm there on time or no job. Thanks all the same, but I'll just take my pay and a full grubsack, if that's OK?'

Larrabee hesitated, then nodded. 'Suit yourself.'

A week later Ben Dodge rode into Boulder, a mite overwhelmed by the traffic and crowded boardwalks. But he had money in his pockets that would see him through until he found a job that suited him, and enough left over for a few drinks and maybe a leeetle wingding tonight. . . .

He stalled his horse, a pale-coloured gelding he called 'Sandy', and the hostler said he could leave his saddle and other gear in the stables, no charge.

He was just wiping trail dust off his Winchester when he heard someone at the entrance to the room where he had been told to stack his gear. A tall, wide-shouldered man, he turned quickly and one of his shoulders brushed the bedroll he had slung temporarily by a rope on a nail. It fell but he made no attempt to catch it, obviously he didn't want to lose his grip on the Winchester.

The rifle in his hand seemed to lift of its own accord across his chest, his right hand slipping over the gooseneck of the stock until his right index finger rested on the trigger. Ready for action.

The man in the doorway, dressed in creased and not-too-clean range clothes straightened, lifted a hand.

'Sorry. Didn't mean to startle you.'

Dodge stared back, saying nothing, but a slight frown appeared between his eyes. That rawboned face. . . .

'Seen you ride in. How's Lacy Corliss these days?' The man grinned as Dodge tightened his grip on the rifle. 'You were in his division at the Red Rock, weren't you?'

Dodge kept staring, his frown deepening. Then suddenly his eyes widened. 'Pinney! I thought you drowned!'

'Damn near did, but got throwed up under a cutbank. Stayed put while they searched – near give myself pneumonia, but they gave up before I did and I crawled out. Never figured to see you walk outta the pen, not the way that son of a bitch Corliss went after you.' Pinney stepped forward, right hand thrust out. 'I'm known as Rusty Rankin around here. Good to see you again, Jarrett.'

Dodge changed the rifle to his left hand and gripped with Pinney.

'Ben Dodge is the name. We better have a drink – er – Rusty. We must be two of a kind, eh?'

Pinney grinned wider. 'Yeah. Only two of less than a handful who made it outta Red Rock pen, alive.'

Dodge sobered as he added, 'And, speaking for myself, who don't aim to go back!'

'Amen to that!'

The first thing he saw when the morphine and other drugs wore off, and the giddy mists had cleared, was a bearded face staring down at him. . . .

'My God!'

Teeth flashed through the beard and the shaggy head moved side to side. 'Afraid not, *amigo*. But I'm sure his hand has guided you here – with a little help from Asa Langdon and friends.' A hand reached over the edge of the casket and fumbled at his side, lifting Jarrett's right hand, finding a firm grip. 'Doctor Morgan Tresize at your service.'

Dave Jarrett tried to sit up but Tresize pressed him back gently. 'Easy, friend, easy. You'll be woozy for quite some time. Be best if you get some more or less natural sleep now, let it all get out of your system.'

Jarrett did, in fact, feel dizzy; he clung to the sides of the confining coffin and blinked at the doctor. 'I – I'd like to – change – beds. . . .'

Tresize laughed, the sound like a small explosion in room. 'That can be arranged. I'll get someone to help.'

Next time he opened his eyes he wished he hadn't.

Bright light slashed at his vision and there was a thudding pain in his head that threatened to explode his skull.

He moaned aloud and someone appeared beside him, standing between him and the brilliant sunlight coming through the window. He squinted, then widened his eyes; it was a woman standing there, reaching out with a small, soft hand and touching his stubbled face. With her other hand she thrust a large tin bowl at him.

'I think you may need this.'

To his embarrassment, he did – immediately, his body being racked by the retching spasms. When he had finished she wiped his mouth with a clean cloth soaked in cool water, took the bowl and set it on a nearby table.

'You'll start to feel better now, but don't expect to be back to normal – or whatever you regarded as "normal" in that dreadful prison – for a few days.'

'I'm – obliged – ma'am.'

'You can call me Gloria – or Mrs Tresize, if you wish to be formal.'

'I reckon I should call you "Angel".'

She laughed, a warm, appealing sound, her face lighting up with genuine pleasure. 'Well, I don't think there's any doubt that you're going to come good in record time!'

'Where am I?'

'A town called Dewey. It hardly appears on any maps, it's so small, which we find to our advantage, considering the kind of . . . work we do.'

He suddenly thought of something. 'Doc Langdon. You hear anything of him, Gloria? He was mighty sick as I recall.'

She sobered. 'Asa Langdon died the night of the same day you were shipped out.' She made a swift sign of the cross with her right hand. 'May the Lord take him into his care.'

'Yeah. Too bad there ain't more folk like him in the world.'

'Well, we'll turn you loose very soon and perhaps you'll see what you can do. . . ?'

'That was about a month back,' the man now calling himself Ben Dodge told Pinney, alias Rusty Rankin, in a quiet corner of the saloon that the latter had brought him to.

'Funny, I'd heard a whisper that Doc Langdon was involved in cuttin' up cadavers. Never thought much about it.'

'Highly organized – thank God. They sure treated me well, doctored all my hurts, fed me mighty fine grub, outfitted me. Just came and asked: "What would you like when you leave, Mr Jarrett? Just tell us what kind of weapon, any preference for a mount, and so on".' He moved his head wonderingly. 'Dunno as I'll ever be able to repay 'em.'

'They wouldn't expect it, would they?'

Dodge looked hard at Pinney. 'I'd expect it. I square my debts.'

Pinney shrugged. He was a big man, with a big face, clean-shaven though showing early signs of a stubble,

29

sandy-haired, with the clearest blue eyes Dodge had ever seen. He had been quiet enough in the pen and it had come as a surprise to most folk when he had somehow busted out – alone. (That part was no surprise, for Pinney was plainly a loner.)

Which made Dodge wonder why the man had sought him out. They hadn't been friends in the pen; not enemies, either, which under the circumstances, might stand in for a kind of friendship. Then: 'How'd you recognize me?' He absently touched his thick moustache as he asked.

'Way you walk, throw out that left foot a mite. I was still there when Corliss busted your ankle with that axe handle. You'll take that limp to the grave, and that moustache draws attention to your face; best be rid of it.'

Jarrett nodded. 'Yeah. How come you're not a lot further south by now?'

Pinney smiled wryly. 'Well, there was this widow woman in Smoke Bend . . .' for a moment his eyes were dreamy. 'Man! An' I mean *woman*! Helluva hard thing to leave her, but had to in the end. Too many others wanted to take my place – one couple were gettin' right het-up about it.'

Dodge smiled. 'What've you been working at?'

'This and that.' Pinney's eyes settled on Dodge's face. 'What made you pick on Ben Dodge for a name?'

Jarrett took a long minute answering, drained his beer before he said, 'I found this dead man. Up in the Dreary Mountains . . . *way* up, above snowline. He'd been throwed by his horse, it looked like, landed on a rock head first. I went through his gear, being short of ammunition and grub and everything else. Found an army jacket and some other stuff, includin' a few sticks of very sweaty dynamite.'

'Whoa! Once them sticks start sweatin', so do I! Mighty dangerous stuff to handle at that stage. What'd you do with it?'

'Buried it deep as I could in the snow, laid Dodge alongside and rode out. Later I checked the jacket pockets and found an army discharge in the name of Captain Ben Dodge. I figured it would be mighty handy to have such identification for any law that might show interest in me. I knew Ben Dodge wasn't gonna show up and say I was using his name . . .' he spread his hands. 'And here we are.'

Pinney nodded as he stood up, took both glasses and went to the bar. When he came back, he set the beer down, then returned to the bar and came back with two shots of whiskey.

'Better drink that – you're gonna need it.'

Dodge looked up at Pinney, puzzled. 'Why?'

'Guess you did'nt know Dodge was a hunted man.'

'What!'

'Yeah – the army and the law; it'd be better and safer for you if it was *only* the law. And there's a whole slew of murdering sons of bitches who've got no use for the damn law but who want to catch up with anyone callin' themselves Ben Dodge.'

Jarrett found his belly knotting. 'What the hell'd he do?'

'Let's put it this way: the men who want him aim to

31

make him tell where he hid a strongbox he stole. They mightn't kill him when they catch up, but they will in the end – and it'll be a long day's dyin'. Me? I reckon I'd change my name pronto! I mean, no one's gonna be lookin' for anyone called Dave Jarrett, are they? He died way back when, before he'd even left Red Rock pen.'

He lifted his whiskey in salute, then tossed it down his throat, grinning as he looked steadily at Jarrett. 'Happy resurrection!'

CHAPTER 4

HONOUR/DISHONOUR

This was how it had started . . . five years earlier. . . .

Captain Ben Dodge, all six-feet-one of battle-active soldier, paused just inside the batwings, and almost immediately saw Cadell through the eye-stinging fug of the saloon's gaming room.

The son of a bitch! Lounging back in his chair, studying his hand of cards, ready to make his killing.

There'll be a killing, all right, you bastard! But not the kind you're hoping for! For starters, I'll change that handsome face to something even the cats wouldn't fight over.

Dodge strode through the crowd, walking straight ahead, straight-arming anyone in his way, thrusting them to one side. He stepped around the house-man who was sitting smugly across the table from Cadell, thumbs hooked in the armholes of his fancy vest, awaiting the player's bet. Then Dodge's big right fist smashed into the middle of Cadell's face like a jack-hammer.

There was a brief squishing sound and the man went over backwards taking the chair with him, cards flying like oversized snowflakes. Trousered legs rose above table level as Cadell struck the sawdusted floor, blood smearing his ruined face. The other gambler shot to his feet, instinctively reaching for his gun under his arm. Dodge grabbed him by the collar and yanked him forward violently, bringing up his knee. The gambler lifted two feet off the ground, gave a strangled scream, and then Captain Ben Dodge – wearing civilian clothes so as not to dishonour the uniform of the United States Cavalry – hurled him aside, kicked a chair away, overturned the table which had already been abandoned by the other card players, and stomped on the man writhing about the floor.

'Here I am, just like I promised, Cadell, you wife-stealing bastard! And here's what I brought you!'

Cadell's head was rolling loosely on his neck, his nose a shapeless blob under all the blood smearing his face, teeth protruding through his mashed bottom lip, one eye already closed. It was doubtful whether he even recognized Dodge, or that he felt the big fist that drove his midriff back against his spine. His supper and the booze he had swallowed afterwards exploded over Dodge and enraged him even more, if that were possible.

Dodge grabbed Cadell by the throat, lifted him

clear off the floor and hurled the flailing man on to the bar top.

By that time the saloon bouncers were closing in. A hardwood billy smashed into Dodge's left shoulder, numbing his arm momentarily. But he spun, instinctively swinging his right arm, knuckles taking the bouncer across one ear as the man set himself for the blow that would knock the officer unconscious.

As the big man sagged Dodge turned quickly, knowing the chucker-outs always operated in pairs. He used his forearm to parry the descending club, kicked the man in the shins, then grabbed him by collar and trouser belt and ran him head first into the bar front. The bouncer went limp and was deposited carelessly on to the brass footrail as someone yelled, 'Watch out! *Gun!*'

Men scattered and dived for the floor. Taken by surprise, Ben Dodge turned, stumbled, put his back against the bar.

Cadell had rolled off the counter and recovered sufficiently to drag his gun from its fancy leather holster. He fumbled the hammer back and was using his only good eye to line up the barrel on Dodge's sweating face, when Ben Dodge reached for his own Colt which he carried merely thrust into his trouser belt; an army holster with a clip-over flap was no way to tote a gun a man might want to use in a hurry.

'No guns!' yelled the barkeep but dropped out of sight behind the counter as both weapons roared.

Dodge staggered and Cadell lurched upright, triggering again. On the floor now, Dodge jammed his elbow against the wet sawdust for support and got off two more fast shots, thumbing the hammer in a practised blur.

Cadell shuddered, took a single wavering step forward, and crashed face down amongst the shattered table and chairs.

Dodge swayed, blood dripping from the fingers of his left hand, his shirt sleeve bullet-torn above the elbow. His own smoking gun was now held down at his right side. The room began to come alive again, though most men were warily watching the soldier-out-of-uniform; they all knew who he was.

Then an army sergeant, Pat Pinney, shouldered his way through and grabbed the captain's right arm, using his left hand to catch the falling Colt and ram it into his own waistband.

'Let's go, Cap! Gonna be hell to pay over this night!'

Dodge shook his buzzing head to clear it and looked into his sergeant's sober face.

'At your – command – Sergeant,' he slurred, the pain of his wound getting to him now.

As the crowd gathered around the dead man Pinney led the captain away, fumbling at his neckerchief, ready to bind the arm wound when there was a chance.

'Jesus!' a man kneeling by Cadell said, shaking his head. 'Dead as last Sunday's breakfast!'

Someone whistled softly. 'Wait'll his old man finds out!'

'I'm glad my name ain't Ben Dodge!'

*

The colonel stood at the full-length window in his office and stared out across the busy parade ground of Fort McNally, hands clasped behind his back. He was ramrod straight, uniform immaculate, grey-streaked hair pomaded and neatly combed. He spoke without turning.

'You've ended your career, of course, Captain.'

His voice was deep without expression: merely making a statement. Standing at attention across the room, left arm in a sling, his own uniform wrinkled and drab in contrast to his commanding officer's, Dodge nodded, cleared his throat and said,

'I realize and regret that, sir.'

'Too bad you didn't give it more thought before you acted last night.'

'I did, sir. That's why I went in civilian clothes.'

The colonel snapped his head around, and the knuckles whitened on his clasped hands. 'Yes! Premeditated. But I will admit that not wearing your uniform was a good thought! Did you set out to kill Cadell?'

'I – I'm not sure, sir. You know he ruined my marriage. I was raging and – well, I'd had a few drinks. I didn't much care about consequences.'

'You should have! Dammit, man, Lyall Cadell, son of the biggest cattle buyer in this State! I've no need to tell you that Cadell senior is after your head.' Dodge remained silent. 'He demands a full-rigged court martial and you know what that means! Bad, *bad*

37

publicity! Bad for the army, worse for you. A death sentence is – probable.'

'Pardon, sir, but there were plenty of witnesses who saw Cadell draw first.'

'The same witnesses who would have to give evidence that you provoked him by your attack!'

Dodge remained silent. The colonel strode back behind his desk, yanked his chair out and stood leaning on its back a few seconds before seating himself. He shuffled some papers, glanced at them briefly, raised his burning eyes to Dodge's stiff, bruised face.

'One way out. I'll allow you to resign your commission, effective immediately, and you will leave Fort McNally *and this State* at all speed.'

Dodge swallowed, fought to keep his face blank.

'Sir, I'm grateful for your leniency, but – I must ask about my – gratuities, pension and so on. . . .'

'Forfeited.'

Dodge heaved a sigh. 'I could salvage what's left of my marriage if I were able to draw them, sir—'

'Forfeited! And be grateful – or Cadell senior may well get his damn court martial.'

Ben Dodge allowed himself to slump a little. 'All right, sir, I'll resign. I feel I'm getting a raw deal, but I'd like to stress that all Sergeant Pinney did was try to get me out of that saloon before there was more trouble.'

'Pinney's discharge papers are already in the system.'

'By God, sir! That's not fair!'

The bleak eyes settled on Dodge's angry face. 'I will have my clerk make out your resignation and you will receive a flat honorable discharge, without comments or recommendations. It's the best I can offer, Ben. Don't resist or you'll push me into a totally untenable position.'

Dodge remained silent, then nodded jerkily.

'I'll sign as soon as the clerk has the papers ready, sir.' His tone was clipped, face tight and pale.

The colonel sighed.'By God, the Army's going to miss you, Ben!'

The noise of the saloon seemed to have increased as Pinney paused to drain his beer. Dave Jarrett stood and went to the bar for refills for both of them.

'Sounds like Dodge was lucky this colonel had a soft spot for him.'

Pinney snorted. 'Not too soft. Dodge needed that pension and the other gratuities he was entitled to. He tried to fix his marriage but his wife was a crazy man-chaser. Ben was about the only one who didn't realize it. Anyway, she cleared out when he couldn't come up with any decent money, and that was when he changed . . . for the worse.'

After fifteen long years of distinguished service the army had let Ben Dodge down. Some would say he had brought it on himself but he was in no mood to shoulder any of the blame. He was broke, thanks to Giselle and her flighty ways. She had even cleaned out his pockets before leaving; went off with some damn drummer from Kansas City: *Oh, Giselle! Surely you could do better than that!*

Before the trouble with Cadell Dodge had been organizing the delivery of a railroad payroll due at end-of-track by the last day of the month; it was only $3,000 or something less, but they wanted an army escort. Ben knew the timetables, the route to be taken, the fact that there was only one shotgun guard, who was past retiring age. They were depending on the escort for the last leg of the delivery through Indian country: just taking normal precautions.

Dodge's plan was for the escort to meet the pay-wagon at a river crossing; he didn't think the colonel would make any changes at this late stage.

So he went looking for Pinney, and found him swinging a pick on the site of the new town hall, and hating every driving blow of it for the pittance he was being paid.

'Walk away, Pat,' Dodge told him. 'Drop that lousy pick and *walk away now!* I'm gonna make you rich.'

'A sawbuck'd make me richer than I am right now,' panted Pinney; he glanced at the surly foreman and threw the pick in his direction. Startled, the man jumped back, glared. 'All yours, Harmon. I forget where it's s'posed to go but I can make a suggestion if you want.'

'You're fired, Pinney!'

Both Pinney and Dodge laughed as they walked off to where Dodge had tethered two horses among the trees. Pinney stopped and stared at the rifle in the saddle scabbard, the six-gun in its holster on the bullet belt hanging over the horn, a bedroll and bulging saddle-bags.

'So, there is a good fairy after all! I had to sell all my gear after they booted me outta the troop.'

'This is yours now.' Dodge paused, looking levelly at his ex-sergeant. 'Courtesy US Cavalry, except the rifle.'

Pinney paused as he examined the Winchester, glanced up at Dodge. 'Remembered that railroad payroll, did you?' He grinned tightly as Dodge raised his eyebrows. 'Been givin' it some thought too.'

'Then I don't have to waste time convincing you: the army owes us. Let's go collect. The Fannin brothers're waiting at Balsam Creek.'

Pinney stopped in mid-step. 'That scum? Hell, we don't need them, Cap!'

Dodge shook his head. 'Might do. They're fighters.' Pinney frowned. 'Don't worry about 'em, Pat. I reckon the colonel will still use my plan. The escort's s'posed to join the wagon at Ryan's Ferry.' Pinney started to show some understanding now and smiled as Dodge added, 'Only *we'll* arrive a day early. Hope you've still got your old uniform?'

'So happens I stashed one away for the winter.'

'That'll get us to the wagon; don't see any need for trouble.'

Pinney wasn't altogether convinced but couldn't help chuckling. 'The colonel would've been better off just payin' out our gratuities!'

Ben looked really mean, surprising Pinney. 'The goddamned piker! Wasn't his money. I need it for Giselle.'

41

'We-ell . . . better than a court martial, I guess.' Dodge only scowled and Pinney asked, 'What's the split? I mean, the Fannins are greedy sonuvers.'

Dodge spoke flatly, in a hard tone Pinney hadn't heard before – altogether different from his parade ground manner, and his easy-going way with the men. 'I'll see the Fannins right.'

Whatever 'right' meant, thought Pinney worriedly. . . .

The deal got out of hand, right from the start.

The colonel, playing it safe, had ordered the armed troopers to join the wagon early, taking the place of the retired shotgun guard. So the escort would already be with the wagon when it arrived at Ryan's Ferry, something they hadn't planned originally. . . . It meant that Dodge's idea, to impersonate the 'escort', would no longer work. But there was no turning back at this stage.

They arrived at the ferry early and edgy; the Fannins were already swilling booze, eager for trouble.

Pinney would rather have let things be, but Dodge wanted that payroll, hell or high water. And he aimed to have it.

Old Man Ryan was a tough, grizzled river man with two sons who were well on the way to emulating their father. He met Dodge's group as they came out of the trees on the southern side of the river. He was holding a long-barrelled Greener, both hammers cocked. His sons, Stew and Johnny, lounged near the thick rope cable and pulley-wheels that would haul the ferry over, each casually holding a rifle.

'Howdy, Ben,' Ryan said, spitting a stream of tobacco juice into the muddy water, squinting. 'Din' expect you'd be in uniform. Heard you an' the army parted ways.'

Pinney looked sharply at Dodge, uneasy now, but Ben shrugged, spoke amiably enough, ignoring the remark about the uniform. 'Thought we might buy a jug of that liquid lightnin' you boys make, and take it along for old time's sake. Can share it till the wagon gets here.'

'Old times are finished for you, Ben; the wagon's already picked up its escort at Halliday's Station. Colonel's orders – takin' extra precautions, I guess . . . or not trustin' you.' He spat again, looked hard at Dodge. 'Since when you hook up with the likes of them Fannin sons of bitches, anyway?'

'Since now, you sassy old bastard!' snapped Cres, the older Fannin, the one with the hair-trigger temper.

He backed his words with a blast from his Colt which he had been holding down at his side away from Ryan. The ferryman staggered back and dropped his Greener. It exploded, leaping into the air. Ryan's boys, briefly stunned, lifted their rifles. Dodge watched it all happening, blowing up in his face, and knew there was nothing he could do about it.

'Wait!' he yelled anyway – he had to try! – but it was too late.

Ryan's sons shot Cres Fannin out of the saddle. He was flung violently into the tree he had stopped beside. His limp body cannoned off and flopped into the river, already choking on his own blood. Walt, the younger Fannin, swore obscenely and cut loose with his pistol. Johnny Ryan spun violently, crashed to the ground, writhing.

Stew Ryan matched Walt's obscenities and triggered even as the young Fannin swung his gun with the speed of a striking rattler and got off two shots. One took Stew high in the chest and by then Walt Fannin was toppling from his horse, which shied away, cannoning into Dodge's mount, throwing his aim as he triggered his rifle. Not that it mattered: Walt was dead before he hit the ground.

Pat Pinney, stunned by the suddenness of the gunfire, held the rifle hammer under his thumb and slowly eased it down. His face was tight and grim as he looked through the gunsmoke at the dead and dying.

'Judas wept, Ben! This wasn't s'posed to be! What happens now?'

Dodge shook his head, squinting through the gunsmoke. He didn't answer at first, then said coolly,

'First rule of warfare, Pat: Improvise pronto when things go wrong. You oughta know that. So, first, we hide the Fannins' bodies: they're no loss. Then we doctor Old Man Ryan and anyone else still living. Both his boys seem to be breathing. Then we wait for the ferry.'

Pinney continued to frown. 'The colonel's men'll know somethin's wrong. The ferryman, too, likely.'

'We gotta convince 'em otherwise.'

'Ye-ah – well, no more killin', for Chris'sakes.'

'Hell, no. The escort'll be busy with their horses

anyway; they nearly always get spooked, way the current pushes the ferry around, and while they're dancin' about, we stop hauling the ferry in.'

'What? Strand 'em in mid-river!'

'That's it – and they stay there till they throw their guns over the side and do what we tell 'em.'

'Christ, they might try to swim ashore!'

Dodge looked steadily at Pinney. 'That's a risk we'll have to take. Not likely they can swim that far, anyway.' Dodge spoke unconcernedly and Pinney felt his belly knot.

He shook his head slowly. 'Never thought I'd see the day you'd turn so callous, Ben! Hell, you *always* gave a man a break!'

'And look where it got me,' Dodge said bitterly, watching Stew Ryan struggling to sit up, blood on his shirtfront. 'This is the one chance to get something out of the damn army, Pat. It's not much, but it's gotta do! I've been wronged, and this way I can partly set things right. I'm trying to square things for you, too, you know.'

Pinney frowned, face tight, obviously uncertain.

'There's no other way now, Pat. No point in abandoning it after this. . . .' Dodge swept a hand around at the sprawled men. 'It's Cres Fannin's doing, anyway; we didn't start it – but to walk away now . . .' He shook his head violently. 'Just wouldn't make sense.'

Pinney clamped his mouth tightly, then nodded jerkily. 'Let's get these fellers doctored, then.'

In the saloon, Pat Pinney paused for a long time after he reached that part of his story.

Jarrett gestured to the the near-empty beer glasses as the noise of the bar closed in around them and the thick tobacco smoke made their eyes water, rasped their throats.

Pinney shook his head. His face showed discomfort at the memory of Ryan's Ferry. 'Old Ryan and Stew pulled through. Both Fannins and Johnny Ryan didn't make it. We buried 'em an' done what we could for the others while we waited for the wagon and the ferry to appear across the river. Ryan's regular ferryman, that one-eyed feller they call "Patch", was there, ready to bring 'em over. Dunno what he thought about all the shootin'; we knew he'd tell the wagon driver and the guards. But they couldn't cross the river anywhere else for ten miles, so we figured they'd come over anyway, find out for themselves.'

'Must've reckoned there'd been trouble and they could be riding into more of the same,' Jarrett allowed.

'Sure. But if they just saw two of us, now wearin' our old uniforms, we figured they'd come in. . . .'

'And they did?'

'Yep. Drove the wagon on to the ferry and Patch started hauling. The soldiers stood up front, rifles ready, and I guess the driver had his shotgun handy. They knew somethin' was up but just had to cross and find out what; no other way to do it.' He smiled crookedly. 'Then we put the brakes on the cable! Stopped 'em dead in the water, smack in the middle.

Ben told 'em to throw their guns overboard and we'd bring 'em the rest of the way. Then we let 'em see we had Old Ryan and Stew as hostages.'

'Hostages!' Dave sounded grim.

'We wouldn'ta harmed 'em, but those payroll boys din' know that, so, after a little argument their guns went overboard.

'One guard had kept a hideaway gun but only had it half-drawn when the ferry finally bumped into the landing. Dodge jumped on to the platform and clubbed him with the rifle butt.

'We made them carry the strongbox ashore, and wondered why the men made such an effort out of it because it looked a lot smaller than we'd expected, but then there was only three thousand dollars in notes and a handful of change.'

Pinney laughed as he came to this part of his story. 'We hustled 'em back on board, Old Ryan and Stew as well, then Ben and me hauled the ferry out and when it was in midstream we cut the cables.'

Jarrett's fingers whitened as he tightened his grip around his glass. 'You cut 'em adrift?'

'The ferry spun around a few times, but the weight of the wagon kept it stable. It was swept out of sight in no time. We knew Old Ryan, wounded or not, would get 'em safely ashore downstream.'

'You did this for three thousand lousy dollars! And how many dead and wounded?'

Pinney's amusement faded at the disapproval in Jarrett's voice and on his face. 'Take it easy, Dave. OK, mebbe it was risky cuttin' the ferry adrift but we had to do it. We needed the time to get away. And it worked out OK.'

'Still took a helluva chance.'

'Told you Ben had changed. I'd been his sergeant for so damn long that I just automatically did what he said. Not makin' excuses – I needed that money and was willin' to do most anything for it. You want a surprise?'

'I've had my surprise! The way it grew into a near massacre from a simple: "*Grab a handful of sky and toss down your strongbox!*" That's all it should've took.'

'Ben was in charge and he didn't like the idea of going up agin hardcase guards like the colonel had chosen – we wasn't tryin' to harm 'em. We knew there'd be half the territory after us if we did.'

'Did you open the strongox?' Dave asked curtly.

Pinney had that half-smile on his face again now. 'Hell, yeah.' He rolled and lit a cigarette; Jarrett noticed his hands were shaking. 'Listen, Dave, the army done us wrong and it was the only way we could get a grubstake.'

'Not the only way. But leave that. You get your share?'

Pinney's mouth tightened. 'Never did. Thing was, when we opened the strongbox it was crammed with money.'

'Small bills for the pay packets, I guess.'

'That's what we thought, too. Until we took out a couple packets and noticed the bank wrappings: hundred-dollar bills, fifties, even one pack with thousand-dollar bills – first we'd seen. Under the top layer it was crammed with gold coins: cold, hard cash!'

He paused, then added, 'Total came to just over seventy thousand bucks!'

CHAPTER 5

WRONG MOVE

Dave Jarrett, face suddenly frozen, digested that – or
tried to.

'Was it real?'

'Yep. Gen-u-ine US currency.'

'Seventy *thousand*! Where the hell was all that
going? Not to any railroad end-of-track.'

Pinney smiled crookedly. 'If I told you, you would-
n't believe it.'

'Hell, I don't believe it now! Who'd ship that much
cash on some backwoods freight wagon, only carrying
back pay for a team of gandy-dancers and track-
layers?'

Pinney's mouth was taut now. 'Try the railroad
company itself, with a couple of land agencies, and
more than a few big-time Montana Cattlemen's
Associations. All interested in right of way, open
range, good grass and high profits – depending on

which land Congress gazetted for such use.'

Dave suddenly jerked up his head. 'Pay-off! Graft and bribe money! For the politicians who can arrange release of the land these men want to exploit!'

'Nicely put, Dave. Ben figured the same – said he'd worked as a bank guard once and stumbled on the same sorta thing. Recognized it right away . . . and there's the rub. Ben went crazy over all that cash. Said he could get Giselle back for sure now. I tell you, no matter how much he cussed her, he was still smitten. Pussy-whipped, I guess.'

'What was your share to be?'

'We agreed right from the start, we'd split anythin' we got fifty-fifty. That was before Ben brought in the Fannins, and sure as hell before we found the bonanza.'

His voice drifted off and Jarrett knew what had happened. 'But suddenly Dodge didn't want to split?'

There was a tremor in Pinney's voice, hurt in his eyes. 'He went off his head. All he could see was that damn woman. Couldn't stop talkin' about her, how they'd travel, live it up like she wanted.' He spat suddenly. 'Damn fool! She'd go through that money like water through a strainer, then dump him. I tried to tell him.'

Pinney's voice quavered as he told how Dodge's big fist had crashed into his ribs and driven him to his knees. Dodge lifted a brutal knee into his face, kicked him repeatedly. He twisted fingers in Pinney's sandy hair, and jerked his bloody face towards the sun. He spoke very deliberately, a crazy look burning in his eyes.

51

'You – keep – your – filthy – mouth – off – *her*!'

Again, Pinney paused in his story, sweat now beading his pinched features.

Dave could see the painful memory on that skull-like face as Pinney said, barely above a whisper:

'He – he picked me up and threw me off the cliff where we had our camp. I was banged up mighty bad and when I came round, he'd gone. With the strong-box.'

'How'd you get out?'

'An Injun, b'lieve or not! Huntin' puma. I thought I was dead for sure. But he splinted my legs, stripped bark off a tree and wrapped it round my ribs. I dunno how he got me out and back to his tribe, but they nursed me till I could ride again. Took about ten weeks.'

'The bloodthirsty red man, eh?' Dave commented. 'Always kill white men on sight . . . so they tell you.'

'Yeah. Makes you think, don't it?'

'You been looking for Dodge?'

'Yeah, mostly. Tried to finance myself by stickin' up a stage. That's how I came to be in Red Rock pen.' Pinney frowned suddenly, threw out his arms. 'But you said you found Ben dead in the Dreary Mountains! So I guess the money's gone for ever. *Goddammit*!'

'Mebbe. But how about this: what was Dodge doing in those mountains?'

Pinney went very still, remained silent for a spell. 'Judas! He could've been stashing the strongbox! Then his horse throwed him. By hell, Dave! We might still have a chance of finding it! Did you see any sign of a mule?'

    'There was a skeleton, coulda been a mule.'

    'The strongbox was on a mule when Ben left!'

    'Hell of a lot of country to search, Pat.'

    'You got anythin' better to do?'

    'Well, now you mention it. . . .'

Chet Larrabee lit his cheroot and folded his arms across the top rail of the corral. He took the cheroot from between his lips and pointed it at the big buckskin stallion standing like a statue in the middle of the pen, head proud, eyes challenging.

'I'm damn sorry to see him go, Hank,' Larrabee said to the man sweating in the frock-coat and vest beside him.

'He hasn't "gone" yet. Not till we dicker some.'

Larrabee arched his bushy eyebrows, looking surprised. 'Dicker? Man, I'm scratchin' rock bottom now. He's a fine-lookin' bronc, as you can see.'

'I can see,' the potential buyer said curtly. 'Don't like the look in his eye. Needs a little more bit-sawin' and some buck-jumpin' with big rowells, I reckon, before he'd be safe to ride.'

'Judas, man, you don't break 'em in by givin' 'em a sore mouth and bloody flanks! You oughta know that – Aaaagh! You're joshin' me! Hank, he's safe as houses! Why, the feller who broke him in had him eatin' outta his hand. I mean it! Handful of grain and that big buck snapped it right up.'

'And now they call him 'Lefty', eh?' the buyer said sceptically. 'A sweet-talkin' bronc-buster, huh? Sounds like he's half-horse himself.'

'Well, that could well be. I seen him talkin' into that stallion's ear while them eyes were rolling and the big teeth were showin'. He settled down quicker'n you could snap your fingers, let Ben tweak his ear, even.'

The buyer grinned. 'You been practising your sales talk, Chet ! Kinda thing I'd say. Anyway, who is this horse-breaker with the magic touch?'

'Dunno as you'd know him. He just drifted in. Name of Ben Dodge, ex-army man. Cavalry, o' course.'

'No-ooo, can't say I've heard of him, but if he was cavalry at least he ought to know which end of a horse you don't try to tweak.'

A beard-shagged man in a sweaty checked shirt, who had been repairing a split nubbing post in the next corral, stood up suddenly and walked across.

'Yeah, well, like I been tellin' you, he knows his hosses and—'

'Where is he now? This Ben Dodge, I mean.'

Larrabee frowned, stopped in mid-sentence, swung his shaggy head around to look at the man in the checked shirt, 'This is a private conversation, mister.'

The buyer stepped back a little, not liking the way the man in the checkered shirt kind of set his shoulders and rested his right hand on his gun butt. Larrabee noticed the threatening gestures, too, and frowned more deeply.

'Mister, you're not in this conversation, so if—'

'All I want to know is where I can find Ben Dodge.'

Larrabee licked his lips involuntarily, feeling a coldness in his chest as he saw the barely contained belligerence in this newcomer. His face was flat-planed and his eyes looked mean, like a snake's.

'Well, I can't tell you where he is. He's a drifter. Offered him a job with my outfit, but he just took his fee for bustin' the buckskin and . . . well, I dunno where he went. Into town, I guess, likely stopped at the saloon. Some of my boys might be able to tell you.'

The bearded man swore softly. 'I need to find him – Din' know he was in this part of the country.'

'Mightn't be the man you want,' the buyer said, trying to be helpful, and to get rid of this tough-looking ranny. ' "Ben Dodge" sounds like a common-enough name.'

Agate eyes swivelled to the buyer's face and he felt himself flush. 'That's how it sounds to you, huh, Grissom? Well, it sounds to me like this is the feller we've been lookin' for, for a damn long time. *Too* damn long.'

'Oh? Some others lookin' for Dodge, too?'

The man seemed suddenly wary. 'Few of us used to work together. Fact is, we owe Dodge some money and want to get it squared away.'

And you can believe that if you think there really is a Santy Clause, Larrabee thought, but didn't say so out loud. 'Go ask my crew, down at the third corral. They know all the saloons and they could tell you if Dodge went to any of 'em. Best I can do.'

The bearded man hesitated, like he wanted to argue. But just then sun flashed off the front of a man's shirt as he approached the group: a deputy sheriff, filling in time, giving the horses the once-over.

But the sweaty man didn't want any part of that badge, or the man wearing it. He tugged his battered hat down and nodded curtly.

'I'll check with 'em. Thanks.'

As he walked away Larrabee asked the buyer, 'You know him?'

'Not really. Seen him around town from time to time. Think his name's Luke Handy, or Early, something like that. Someone said once he has kin here.'

'Tough-lookin' *hombre*.' Chet Larrabee heaved a sigh. 'Now, about this buckskin, Hank. You know he's a bargain. . . .'

The tough-looking man, Luke Handy, did have kin in town: his cousin was the telegraph operator, and he hurried to the agency after learning from drinkers in the nearest bar that Dodge had visited a local saloon after breaking in the buckskin stallion for Larrabee. No one was sure which way he'd ridden out of town, later, but it was a start.

'Howdy, Luke,' the telegraph operator greeted the man in the checked shirt. 'You look kinda – excited.'

'You still know how to get in touch with Wallis and Steed, Will?' Luke asked, thumbing back his hat.

The operator, hunched from years at the telegraph key, straightened in his chair. He stared at his cousin, then said, 'Ain't had to call 'em for a spell. But I guess I can try the old place if you want.'

'Do that. Tell 'em to come quick, and to bring that five hundred bucks re-ward.'

Will arched his eyebrows. 'For what?'

'For pickin' up a lead on Ben Dodge!'

Will pursed his lips, rubbed the lobe of his left ear. 'Might have to do a deal of searchin' before I track them gunfighters down, Luke. Like I said, it's been a while and they move around a lot. Could take a while—'

'Yeah, yeah! OK. Fifty bucks if you do it pronto! Provided they bring the re-ward. OK?'

Will grinned, turned to the key and made it sing as he tapped rapidly. . . .

Dave Jarrett and the man calling himself Rusty Rankin left the saloon after their long talk and did a deal with the livery man to allow them to sleep in his loft for the night.

That arranged, they pooled their money and found they had only eleven dollars and some cents between them.

'Ain't gonna get enough stores to see us to the Drearies with that,' averred Pinney.

Jarrett agreed and that afternoon they went down to the lumber yard and found work: stacking undressed timber taken from the saw pit to the planing shed for finishing. Then they worked till sundown loading wagons with dressed lumber ready for pick-up or delivery to people in the county who needed it for the homes they were building.

They worked another two hours by lantern-light, dragging heavy logs in from the flume race ready for debarking in the morning. Then they picked up their money – just short of ten dollars each – and decided they had earned a couple of drinks.

They went to the livery first to wash up in a rain-water barrel.

That was a mistake.

After stripping to the waist and sluicing the icy water over his head, face and upper body, Dave Jarrett dried himself on a flour sack he kept for this purpose. He was rubbing up his hair, Pinney groping for his own towel, when they heard voices. Someone talking to the livery man.

'I bought him in Boulder from Chet Larrabee. He's more or less broke in, but for riding he ought to be gelded. I know John Ketchum up here, best vet in the Territory. So I need a real good stall to keep the buck-skin in for a couple nights. I'm prepared to pay extra and. . . .'

Hank Grissom stopped speaking as Dave Jarrett appeared in the aisle, hair tousled, still stripped to the waist, looking at the big buckskn stallion he had busted for Larrabee. He went straight to the horse; it nodded its head and pawed the ground with one foot.

'Hey, you old jughead! You recognize me!'

Dave stroked the big head and the horse made a playful snap, then allowed him to tweak an ear and talk softly to it. The livery man and Grissom looked at each other, the buyer saying,

'By hell! He wasn't that friendly on the way up here!'

'Ah, he's a mite cussed, but he'll make a damn fine mount once he's gelded. You bought him from Larrabee, you say?'

'Yeah, and by the sounds of it you could be the feller broke him in. Ben Dodge, that right?'

Pinney had arrived by now and he and Dave exchanged a quick glance, the latter seeing no way out of this but admitting to being 'Dodge'. There would be too many explanations – and suspicions – if he said different.

'Yeah, I rode him. Wouldn't say he's fully broke.' He ran his hand under the buckskin's jaw and patted the muscled chest. 'Are you, huh? Just waitin' for some unsuspecting feller to mount up so you can toss him into the next county.'

'There was a man I met in Boulder looking for you,' Grissom said, breaking into Dave's thoughts. 'Said he used to work with you and owed you money. Luke . . . Handy, I think.'

Jarrett thought briefly, shook his head. 'Dunno him. If he owed me money I'd damn sure remember.'

That brought smiles all round and Grissom said, 'Well, that's what he claimed. Larrabee speaks highly of you, Dodge. I travel a lot buying up good horses. Mebbe I could use a man like you to help me select the best?'

Jarrett shook his head. 'Sorry. On my way to a job already. Leaving tomorrow.'

'I could pay generously. I've got a rep for that.'

'I know your rep, Mr Grissom, and it's good all the way, but – no, I've give my word on this other deal.'

Grissom nodded, his disappointment showing. 'Well, I wouldn't ask – or expect – a man to break his word once he's given it. But you ever want a job, look me up. I travel a lot, as I said. But someone'll know where to find me.' He stopped abruptly and said, 'Hey – lemme buy you and your friend a drink. All right?'

They could hardly refuse as they were going to the saloon anyway. Grissom nodded to the livery man.

'You know what I'm after, Jeb. Find a good stall for the buckskin, all right?'

'Got just the thing down the back, Mr Grissom,' the liveryman said, taking the rein in a short grip, feeling the resistance immediately. He looked quickly at Jarrett. 'Mebbe I could ask you to help me get him settled before you go for that drink?'

'Sure,' Dave agreed – after all the man had given him permission to sleep in the loft.

Grissom went on ahead to the saloon and Jarrett and Pinney followed about twenty minutes later.

There was the usual noise and smoke and rowdy drinkers, the tinkling of the battered piano with a tubby, bald man running his hands over the keys, eyes closed, head bobbing to some tune only he was hearing.

Bar girls were circulating. Jarrett and Pinney saw Grissom sitting at a corner table with a bearded man in a checked shirt. Both had beer and shot glasses before them. Pinney jerked his head towards the table.

'Know the feller with Grissom?'

Jarrett shook his head. 'No. But we're going to in a minute.' He smiled briefly and lifted a hand in reply to Grissom's wave, gesturing for them to come over.

Grissom fussed a little, managed to get the attention of one of the bustling, sweating waiters. 'What'll you have? We're on beers and chasers.'

'Fine with us,' Jarrett answered, looking at the man in the checked shirt who was returning his gaze through narrowed eyes.

'By the way, this is Luke Handy. You recall him now?'

Dave shook his head slowly. Handy stood, his big body seeming to tower over the table. He nodded jerkily. 'You're Ben Dodge, so Hank tells me.'

'If I am, you don't owe me any money as I recall,' Jarrett answered slowly.

'Aw, dunno why I said that. Make it like a good reason, I guess. I just wanted to find you.'

'Why?'

'The reasons are kinda . . . private.'

'You come all the way up from Boulder to see me?'

'Well, not exactly. I didn't know you was here. I come to meet a couple of . . . friends, due in on tonight's stage.'

Pinney said, 'Must be in a hurry. The stage continues to Boulder. It'd be there by noon tomorrow.'

Handy's bleak gaze was unfriendly as he settled it on Pinney's face. 'Where and when I choose to meet my friends is my business, mister – and none of yours.'

'Take it easy now,' said Grissom quickly, looking from Handy to the other two men, sensing the mounting suspicion and hostility. 'Let's all have a drink and relax.'

The sweating waiter deposited the drinks and Grissom gave him some money, waving away the change. The man grunted thanks and left. Grissom gestured hopefully at the foaming beer glasses and the brimming shot glasses.

'Let's drink to a good night, eh, gents?'

The tension eased. They sat down and the drinks were tossed down quickly. Dave thought Luke had already had a few – maybe more than a few. Grissom was beaming now.

'How about a hand of cards? Just a friendly game, to fill in the evening?' Hank suggested, then rolled his eyes at a couple of hopeful bar girls hovering near by. 'Or – if your predilection runs to ladies and lace. . . ?'

'Thanks just the same, Mr Grissom,' Jarrett said, standing with his beer in his hand. 'But we'll have the drink and then go turn in. Early start in the morning.'

The horse trader looked disappointed, but sighed resignedly. 'As you will.'

'You boys headed anywhere near Boulder, you're welcome to ride along with me and my friends when I meet 'em,' broke in Luke Handy, trying for a friendly smile, but he couldn't quite make it. He was tense, didn't want to lose sight of 'Ben Dodge' now that he believed he had found him.

'Thanks, but we'll stick to our own schedule.'

Handy's reddened eyes slitted even more. 'You two ain't very friendly. What's the matter?' He looked down at his soiled shirt and trousers. 'My clothes ain't fancy enough? Or is it just that you was a captain too long in the cavalry, Dodge? Makin' men jump when you spoke. Well, I ain't one of your enlisted men, and if you—'

'Forget it, Handy,' cut in Pinney. 'We just don't want

company when we ride out. Nothing personal.'

'The hell it ain't personal!' Handy kicked his chair aside. 'I'm *makin'* it personal!'

He made a move towards his gun. Jarret came across the table in a headlong dive, scattering glasses and drinks, reaching for Handy. No one had expected either move; and Grissom jumped up in alarm, the saloon girls got well clear and Pinney paused as he slapped a hand to his own gun butt.

Jarrett and Handy crashed into the next table, scattering the cursing drinkers, and went down in the midst of splintering wood and shattering glass. Handy squirmed out from under Jarrett and tried to wrench his Colt clear of leather. Dave head-butted him, seeing stars himself, but knowing Luke Handy would have felt like he'd been hit with a jackhammer.

Luke, forehead gashed now, let the gun go and struck out wildly with his left fist. It glanced off Jarrett's ear and sent him staggering, Handy threw himself after him, using his knees and elbows, grabbed for Dave's hair and banged his head on the sawdusted floor. Again Dave saw stars bursting behind his eyes, but instinct cut in and he stabbed upwards with stiffened fingers. They struck Handy in the throat and the man reared up, gagging and choking as he grasped his thick neck, eyes bulging.

Dave rolled away and got to his feet – not bouncing up as he would have liked, slowed some by the knee he had taken in his ribs; they were still weak from Lacy Corliss's tender caresses. But he swayed in and hooked Handy in the big belly, sending the man lurching backwards. He struck the wall and Dave stepped in, spread his boots and hammered a barrage of blows into the other's heavy body.

Luke Handy roared suddenly through his pain and thrust off the wall, coming head down and swinging heavily-muscled arms. Dave was forced to step back and to interrupt his own brutal tattoo. Handy swung a left and when Dave dodged instinctively, had his right fist waiting.

It exploded against the side of Jarrett's head, sending him stumbling towards the bar. Shouting onlookers quickly got out of the way and Dave struck hard. Handy stepped in fast and punched him twice in the kidneys. His legs buckled and he grabbed at the bar top to keep from falling, Luke Handy moved to the side, reached for a bottle and smashed it against the bar edge. There was a roar from the crowd but no one tried to take the brutal weapon away from Luke.

Except Pinney, who made a wild rush in but had to leap swiftly back as the jagged glass slashed at his midriff. It caught the loose folds of his shirt and cut into them. It tangled somehow and, while it only took a few seconds to free, Dave moved in and slammed a fist into the side of Handy's thick neck. It knocked the man halfway along the bar, the broken bottle falling from his grip.

Dave stepped up, placed a hand on the back of Luke's head and smashed the man's face into the edge of the counter.

Everyone within a radius of ten feet heard Luke's nose go. The man flopped wildly for a moment, like a chicken with its head cut off, then fell to his knees. His face was masked in blood. He spat more as he sagged forward and slowly toppled over on to his side.

Jarrett stood over him, fists cocked, but he saw that it was ended and let his hands drop. He swayed and Pinney came up with a bottle of whiskey he had grabbed from somewhere. Dave was short of breath but managed to gulp down a couple of mouthfuls. He let his head hang, chest heaving beneath his torn and blood-spattered shirt. Man, he was plumb tuckered out!

CHAPTER 6

THE HUNTERS

Nash Wallis and Bradford Steed stepped down from the stagecoach into the dimly lit square of cleared ground that served as the arrival area for passengers. The bulk of the stage depot reared behind it, a yellowish glow showing at the windows and doorway.

The two men were well dressed, not flashily, but their clothes were better and cleaner than the average ranny wore this far west. They stood still once they had stepped down, both removing their hats, Wallis's was an unusual shade of dark blue, Steed's was regular grey. They wiped their faces with coloured neckerchiefs.

'Would you kinda mind gettin' outta the way so someone else can get off?'

Steed turned and looked at the unshaven, red-eyed man standing in the doorway of the coach; they had put up with his snores and offensive body odour for many miles and his rough request didn't set easy.

Steed, a man about five-ten, rangy, late thirties, with a horselike face and jutting jaw, looked up at the man.

'You want to get down, friend?'

'That's what you usually do when you're standin' in the doorway like this.'

'Sorry I blocked your way. Come on down.'

He reached up casually, hooked his left hand under the big man's belt buckle and turned quickly, heaving without obvious effort. The big man yelled as he floundered, then found himself airborne for a few moments before hitting the clean-swept ground, stumbling, half-running in an effort to keep his balance. He lost and sprawled untidily in the dust.

Someone gasped in the coach and without looking Steed figured it would be the prissy-looking woman in dusty black with strands of grey hair that kept tumbling out from under her bonnet. The big man skidded, rolled, thrust up with one hand and turned to face Steed. Wallis was busy lighting a slim cheroot, but his hard brown eyes were watching through the match flame.

The big man swore. This brought another gasp of displeasure from the lady in black. And while still cussing, he groped for his six-gun.

'Hell, don't bother, you damn fool,' Steed said in a pleasant voice. 'I could shoot your eyes out before you closed your hand round the butt. C'mon. Forget it.'

'Like hell!' The big man lifted his gun but froze when he saw the Smith & Wesson suddenly appear in Steed's left hand: a crossdraw too fast to see. His tongue licked at his lips and then he saw that the hammer wasn't cocked and Steed's thumb was nowhere near it.

Gaining sudden confidence, he brought up his Colt, anyway, hesitated when Steed's right hand lifted, palm out.

'I'll give you a chance, *amigo*,' Steed said amiably enough. 'You likely haven't seen a gun like this before. I don't have to cock the hammer for each shot. It's what they call a "double-action". When I pull the trigger, it cocks and fires all in the one motion. Fairly new on the market and suits me fine. You want a demonstration?'

The big man swallowed, shook his head slowly; he had heard of these Smith & Wesson innovations, together with their break-action cylinder for fast loading. He nodded, surly, but sensible enough not to push it.

'We could meet again, mister.'

'Not likely, but feel free to step up and say "howdy" if we do.'

Steed even smiled faintly and the big man turned away towards the luggage boot, growling at the driver to find his gear and be quick about it.

Steed touched a hand to his hatbrim and handed down the lady in black, whose face he couldn't see properly because of the thin black veil she wore. 'I beg your pardon for the delay, ma'am. Could I fetch your luggage and carry it somewhere for you?'

The woman stared from behind her veil, surprised, then shook her head and said crisply, 'No, thank you.'

She turned as a younger woman appeared around the corner of the building, obviously having hurried down here to the depot.

'Oh, Aunt Charlotte! I'm sorry. I had a customer in for a fitting and I. . . .' she explained a trifle breathlessly.

'See to my baggage, please, Alexandra,' cut in the woman in widow's weeds, 'And take me to your house. I am in need of a strong cup of tea.'

Wallis, taller than Steed and bulkier, blew a stream of smoke and looked over the young woman. Mid-twenties, he figured, could be a nice body under those clothes: a blouse, with a shawl around her shoulders, hid the top half of her figure, and the skirt that kind of swept out from the waist before falling groundward, did not allow any hip- or leg-line to show. But she was pretty tall for a woman, five seven at least, topped by jet-black hair. Friendly face, no paint that he could see in this light, and a warm smile for her aunt.

'You need a hand with your luggage, ma'am?' Wallis asked, doffing his hat.

Alexandra – 'Alex' – Birdwood looked at him in surprise but before she could answer Aunt Charlotte said,

'I have already refused help from this man's companion. Get a move on, dear. I've had an exhausting journey.'

Alex threw a brief smile of thanks-for-the-offer in Wallis's direction and, followed by the aunt, went to the rear of the coach.

'How long we stayin'?' Wallis asked.

Steed smiled crookedly. 'Just overnight.' He looked around. 'Where's this feller who's s'posed to meet us?

Forgotten his name.'

'Luke Handy. Oh-oh! Could that be him?'

Handy came limping into the light, his battered face and blood-spattered clothes telling anyone with eyes to see that he had been in a tough fight – and recently. He weaved towards the two men, who were now standing a little clear of the bustle around them.

'Wallis and Steed?' he grated.

'*Mr* Wallis and *Mr* Steed – yes,' Steed corrected him soberly.

'Eh? Oh, yeah. Whatever you say. You gents like to follow me, I'll show you to the hotel.'

'Sure you'll be able to walk that far?'

Handy looked at Wallis out of his blackened, swollen eyes. 'I can make it.'

'You been caught in a stampede?' Steed asked, grabbing a roustabout by the arm and slipping him a silver coin. He pointed to the activity at the rear of the coach. 'Two leather valises, initials "B.S." on one, "N.W." on the other. Bring them and follow us.'

'Yessir.' The man glanced at the coin, eyes widening as he saw it was a silver dollar. 'Yes *sir*!' He hurried away, shouldering the driver aside, looking for the luggage.

Handy hadn't answered Steed's question about the stampede and didn't intend to. 'Hope you brought that re-ward money.' They looked at him coolly and he added, 'He's still in town – the son of a bitch.'

Wallis grinned and nudged Steed. 'I think he just answered your question, Brad – it was a one-man stampede.'

Steed nodded but Handy limped along, scowling.

'Very funny! Well, you bring my money?'

'Just take us to the hotel – and it better not be some pig-pen.'

'It's the best in town!'

'Now there's a recommendation for you,' Steed chuckled as they turned into Main Street and saw the light-dappled shadows cast by the frame buildings of the town. 'I can see this is a real prosperous town.'

They glanced around, unimpressed, but they saw the girl, Alex, now carrying a heavy carpetbag, leading her aunt towards a small drapery store. As she set down the bag and fumbled at the door lock they saw, printed in a red arc across the streetfront window, the words:

DRAPERY AND DRY GOODS

Underneath in plain capitals were:

A. BIRDWOOD, PROP.

Then Luke Handy said, 'We cross the street here. That's the hotel, one with the two floors.'

Wallis and Steed exchanged resigned looks, and followed Handy towards the old building. The paint wasn't fresh but at least it wasn't peeling. Maybe the beds wouldn't have bugs.

Alex Birdwood was quite terse with her aunt as she opened the shop door and stood aside for the older woman to step out into the street.

'There's absolutely no need for you to put up at the hotel, Aunt Charlotte! You know you're more than welcome to stay here. It'll only be for a night or two until the Denver stage arrives.'

'Thank you, dear. Very kind of you. But you haven't the room and I will not put you out of your own bed when I can well afford to pay for a hotel room.'

Alex turned to lock the door. 'Father's side of the family always were stubborn,' she muttered and Aunt Charlotte smiled faintly. When Alex turned she jumped, startled, by the two men who had suddenly appeared on the boardwalk. The widow in black clutched her bag more tightly.

Jarrett and Pinney both touched their hatbrims and Dave said, 'Sorry, ma'am. Didn't mean to startle you. Jeb Laycock at the livery noticed our shirts were all tore up . . .' he somewhat embarrassedly indicated his ripped shirt, still spattered with a little of Handy's blood. 'He said you did repairs. We – er – we're kinda short of cash for buyin' new ones and was wonderin' if you could sew up these?'

Alex glanced briefly at their clothing. 'They're pretty badly torn but I can repair them easily enough. I'm closed for the night. Can you come back in the morning?'

'Well – we were kinda hopin' to make an early start,' Pinney explained.

Alex hesitated, then shook her head. 'I'm sorry, I can't do it now and I won't be opening the shop until tomorrow. Come around about eight.' She saw their faces drop and said, 'Oh, well, half past seven if you like. No, I'll tell you what: I'll see my aunt settled in at the hotel and if you like to come back in, say, an hour, I'll do your shirts then.'

They thanked her and moved away. Aunt Charlotte watched them go disapprovingly.

'You should be careful whom you invite into your shop at this time of night, my girl!'

'Oh, they're just the usual cowpoke type, Aunty.'

They moved away and neither noticed the man standing in a doorway of the druggist's, next door to Alex Birdwood's drapery.

It was Luke Handy.

He looked towards the livery; Jarrett and Pinney were just going through the big open doors. . . . *Gonna spend the time in the stables, instead of having a few more drinks, the pikers! OK!*

He hurried towards the hotel, taking the side entrance as Alex and her aunt entered by the front. He hurried up the back stairs and went along to the room he had booked for Wallis and Steed. He knocked lightly on the door, saying in a harsh whisper,

'Lemme in! It's Luke Handy! I got news for you.'

Wallis opened the door, his face set in hard lines. 'The hell you want? We told you, no money till you show us Ben Dodge.'

'Just what I aim to do!' Handy tried to push past Wallis but the gunfighter didn't move, his bulky body effectively blocking Handy. 'I know where he is now – with that pard of his, calls himself Rusty Rankin.'

Wallis's brittle gaze bored into the man's battered

face. 'What you reckon, Brad?' he asked without turning his head.

'Let's hear what he has to say,' Steed said, and Wallis moved aside.

Handy went in swaggering. 'You keep that money handy for ol' Luke Handy, OK!' He chuckled but didn't raise a smile from the two gunmen.

'Hurry it up,' growled Wallis. Luke's smile vanished as he nodded and started to speak in a low voice.

When Dave Jarrett and Pinney entered the stables, Jeb Laycock poked his head out of his cramped office.

'Was hopin' to see you two. Vet Doc Ketchum says he has to go out to one of the big ranches tomorrow – stud mare in some trouble with a foal due – so he wants to geld that buckskin tonight. Can you two take the hoss down to his place and kinda smooth things a little for the doc? I know you're strapped, so I'll pay you five bucks. Sound all right?'

The deal was agreed and they led the stallion by the back lanes to Doc Ketchum's veterinary shed not far from the stables. The vet was all ready with his heavy leather apron tied around his ample waist and gleaming instruments laid out on a couple of frayed towels. He picked up a wicked pair of shears and worked them, the stallion's eyes rolling a little as light gleamed off the metal.

'You boys just do exactly what I tell you as soon as I put him to sleep and then its just *snip!-snip!*' He worked the shears quickly. 'And Bob's your aunty.'

Jeb Laycock swore softly as he lost his place once more adding up the figures in his account book. *Damn!* He sighed, threw down his pencil and stepped out of his office, turning towards the sound of new arrivals.

He stopped and felt a sudden tension knot his belly as he saw the two strangers who had put on the little show at the stage depot.

'Where is he?' Wallis asked.

'Who?'

'Ben Dodge. Calling himself "Jarrett" I heard. He came in with his pard, Rusty someone, a little while ago.'

Jeb licked his lips. 'I dunno about names,' he said carefully, picking these men for troublemakers right off. 'But couple of fellers left twenty minutes or so back.' He pointed through the big doors, 'Rode south towards the mountains.'

Wallis turned to Steed. 'You hear that? He don't know about "names", he says. Reckons them two fellers left already. Well, if they did they ain't the ones we're after.'

Jeb frowned. 'How you know. . . ?'

' 'Cause our good old friend Luke Handy described their mounts. Just like them two in that rear stall.'

Laycock started to back off as they took a step towards him. Then Steed lunged and caught the suspender straps of his grimy coveralls, yanked him back hard enough so the livery man lost his footing. He fell sprawling. Steed, still holding the bib-and-brace front, gave the straps a yank so that they tightened across Jeb's throat. He began to kick as he gagged and made

75

strangling sounds.

Wallis stepped in and whipped the barrel of his Colt back and forth across the man's congested face. Then he kicked him in the stomach and after watching him convulse a few times, dry-retching, he nodded and Steed released Jeb.

Laycock fell full length, half-conscious, rubbing his throat, blood smearing his face.

Wallis leaned over him. 'Now, let's start again. And this time get it *right!*'

He emphasized this last word with another kick and Jeb nodded vigorously.

Then passed out.

'Goddammit! Look at that, Brad! No guts at all.'

'Get a bucket and throw some water over him.'

The water shocked Laycock back to reality – and to all his pains, his face throbbing. He reached up and touched the gashes with trembling fingers.

'That was just a practice run,' Wallis told him, coolly, hefting his six-gun again, flicking a piece of Jeb's bloody flesh from the blade sight. 'Now we start proper. You ready?'

Jeb shook his head slowly. 'They – they went down to the vet's. Square shack, a few hundred yards along the crick. . . .'

He was gasping, ashamed to give in, but afraid these two might kill him, or burn down his livery.

'Now that's showing some sense, eh, Brad?' Wallis leaned forward and patted Laycock's bloody cheek. 'Good work, old man. Now you just rest easy a spell.'

His gun crashed against the liveryman's head and

knocked him sideways, where he sprawled, bleeding and unconscious.

Steed grunted, gesturing to the stall where Jarrett and Pinney had left their gear. 'Good chance to take a look through it. They'll be busy at the vet's for a spell.'

Wallis looked a little uncertain but nodded. He holstered his gun and stepped into the stall, kicking the bedrolls and saddle-bags out into an open space.

They didn't find much of interest until Steed picked up the old army jacket. As he felt the flap pockets he detected the rustle of paper. He unbuttoned the flap, pulled out a square of heavy paper and unfolded it. He read quickly, starting to smile.

Wallis noticed, asked sharply: 'Something. . . ?'

'Yeah. No matter what he calls himself, this ranny is definitely Ben Dodge.' He waved the paper. 'Army discharge in the name of Captain Benjamin Henry Dodge, and so on. Honourable, too, b'lieve it or not.'

'Not true, is it? Man's a liar, not even using his right name.'

Steed continued to smile as he put the discharge paper back into the jacket pocket. 'What about this other feller: Rankin? Seems like they're pards.'

'Ah, might as well kill him. Dodge is the one we need alive. And Handy? We're not going to pay him that five hundred are we?'

Steed pursed his lips. 'Reckon not. Anyway, don't think he'll survive that fall from the second floor of the hotel into the alley.'

Wallis raised his eyebrows. 'Oh? Didn't know about that. When did it happen?'

Steed took a watch out of his vest pocket, flipped open the cover and said, 'About twenty, thirty minutes from now, I'd say.'

Wallis chuckled, then sobered. 'Sad, very sad!'

Jarrett and Pinney finished early at Ketchum's veterinary; the stallion had gone out like a blown match flame when the anaesthetic hit him and Ketchum proved himself to be very adept and even considerate.

'Thank you, gents,' he said, having barely raised a sweat. 'A very easy and successful job, if I do say so. Er – Jeb Laycock arranged some sort of payment, I presume?'

'Yeah, we're fixed up, Doc.' Jarrett gave the sleeping buckskin a parting pat on the head, then they left, making their way to Alex Birdwood's drapery.

She got to work quickly on the torn shirts and admonished the two men: 'These shirts could do with a good wash. But be careful of my stitches, now. Don't be too rough or you'll undo all my work.'

'We'll watch it, ma'am, and thank you.' Jarrett began to pull on his shirt as did Pinney with his faded blue one, which was even more worn than Jarrett's. 'How much we owe you?'

'Oh, it didn't take long and I had some end-of-reel thread. We won't worry about payment.'

They started to protest but she got up and left the room. They finished tucking in their shirts. When she appeared again, she held what looked like a bundle of grey cloth. She shook it out and they saw that she was holding two men's shirts.

78

'A miner ordered these some time ago, but unfortunately he was killed in a rockfall. Why don't you two take them?'

'Well, ma'am, I think Dave told you we're kind of strapped and—'

'Oh, I don't mean you to pay for them. They've been lying around for a few months now. As you can see the cloth is woollen, they were made for the winter. They may be a trifle warm for you now, but they're very durable.'

'Warm don't matter, ma'am,' Pinney said. 'Not where we're goin' – above the snowline.'

Jarrett nudged him quite roughly as he stepped past and said, 'Feel we have to give you something, Miss Birdwood. You must've put a lot of work into those shirts.'

She smiled, a warmth transforming her sober face, blue eyes crinkling. 'You don't understand! This isn't only my work, it's my – how can I put it? It's what I enjoy most in life. Sewing and embroidering, even designing a frock or two. It's . . . pure pleasure for me to make anything at all in fabric. I don't count the time, as long as I produce a finished product I'm happy with and can be proud of.'

'Well, you can be proud of these,' Pinney said, taking one of the shirts and holding it in front of him. 'A mite big, but with Dave's cookin' – and we oughta have plenty of venison in the mountains – I'll soon fill it.'

'That's good. Why don't you try this one on, Mr Jarrett?'

'Dave, ma'am.' Jarrett took off his repaired shirt and shrugged into the woollen one. It prickled his skin a little but fitted well enough, the sleeves being just a smidgen too long. 'I reckon that's fine, ma'am. If you won't take any money, is there something we can do around your shop or the living section? We're handy with tools.'

'Yeah, specially big hammers,' Pinney said with a wink at Steed. The girl looked puzzled but they didn't try to explain.

In the end she found an old heavy dresser she had been meaning to have removed to the yard shed and they did the job for her quickly and efficiently. She could see they were happier then; these were proud men, liked to fulfill their obligations.

They left with her wishes for 'good hunting' in their ears, and made their way back to the stables.

Where they found Jeb Laycock doctoring his injuries.

He told them what had happened, his words slurred because of his swollen and cut mouth.

'Their names are Wallis and Steed,' Jeb finished.

Jarrett looked at Pinney who shook his head: he didn't know them. 'I'll fetch the deputy—'

'No!' Laycock said quickly. He shook his head for emphasis. 'Don't do that; he's out at Will Donovan's spread, anyway: Will's havin' rustler trouble. Besides, our deputy's a young feller, mighty popular, just raisin' a family. These sons of bitches'll kill him soon as look at him. I'll be OK. I've had worse than this.'

Their estimation of the rawhide, lean old liveryman

rose several notches.

'Heard 'em say one of you is called "Ben Dodge",' Laycock told them quietly. 'I was lyin' doggo, didn't let on I was conscious. They're plannin' somethin' for Luke Handy, didn't quite pick up 'xactly what, but they're out-and-out killers, gents. I was you, I'd clear town tonight – in fact, right now!'

That was good advice and they took it.

CHAPTER 7

UNWELCOME VISITORS

Alex Birdwood had removed the drawers from the old dresser when it was moved outside. She was sorting through their contents – old, part-used reels of thread, bundles of near-perished elastic, patterned squares of long-out-of-fashion old fabric called 'fat quarters', some rusted needles and pins, all the worn-out or discarded bits and pieces of her trade, stretching over the ten years she had worked in her own small business.

She picked up a small pincushion that she had made long ago, in the shape of a hedgehog, its quills represented by the pins. She smiled as she remembered when she had made it and how her father had enthused over it as one of her early pieces worth keeping.

Then there was a hammering on the front door and she sighed with a touch of exasperation.

'What's the use of closing the shop and turning out the lamps except for in my living quarters, when half the town keeps finding after-hours work for me!'

She murmured this to herself, as she had done a hundred times in the past, but she really wasn't all that put out. She liked talking about her work whatever the hour and. . . .

Two men stood there: men she recognized from the stage depot, the ones whose offers of help with her luggage Aunt Charlotte had refused. Hard-eyed, dangerous-looking men.

'Yes?' she asked tentatively.

Steed doffed his hat, revealing a mostly bald pate with a few strands of pale hair combed across. Wallis just stood there, thumbs hooked casually in his cartridge belt.

' 'Evenin', ma'am,' Steed said in his best modulated voice. 'Sorry to trouble you, but might we have a word with – er – Mr Jarrett or Mr Rankin? We believe they are visiting you to have some shirts repaired.'

'Oh, you've missed them by quite a long time – an hour at least.'

The men's faces tightened. 'We missed 'em at the veterinary's, too!' Wallis said curtly. 'The doc said they were coming here.'

'Yes, they did. But as I've just said, they've been and gone.'

'Where?' It was only one short word but the clipped way Steed said it caused Alex to tighten her hold on the edge of the door and her breathing to quicken slightly.

83

'I – I have no idea. To get their horses or go to wherever they intended to spend the night, I suppose. *Here*! What d'you think you're. . . ?'

They crowded her back into the shop and Wallis kicked the door closed behind him.

She started to turn and run but Wallis reached out swiftly, grabbed the loose back of her blouse. The sudden tension as she lunged away tore the material and shock and shame made her stop, whip around and hastily grab the front of her blouse to keep it from falling open.

Wallis was close and grinning. 'Aw, don't be bashful, sweetheart! Gimme a look!'

'Nash!' snapped Steed. 'Concentrate on what we're here for.'

'We-ell, when I see a bonus. . . .'

Steed stepped in and knocked his hand away from the wide-eyed girl's clothing. She stumbled back into her cutting-and-sewing room, where a lamp burned. She saw a pair of shears nearby and grabbed, but Wallis intercepted her and twisted her arm behind her. He put his lips close to her ear.

'No time for trouble, sweetie. Just tell us where them two sons of bitches went and we'll leave you alone.' He turned his head and winked at Steed, who was not amused.

'Use your head, lady,' Steed told Alex who was close to tears now, her face ghastly pale. She had stopped struggling, partly to keep her blouse from tearing any more than it already had, but mostly to ease the pain in her arm.

84

'I – I honestly don't know where they are!'

Her rising voice told them she was close to screaming and Steed took one step towards her, poked a stiffened finger into her midriff. It choked off the rising scream and cut off her breath. She floundered, groped for the edge of the table to keep from falling. Wallis viciously knocked her hand away and she fell, striking her head on the edge of the heavy table.

On her knees now, she cried out as Wallis twisted his hand in her plentiful jet-black hair and hauled her to her feet. Her hands groped at his to save her hair being torn from her scalp and he flung her half-across the table. She looked up at him, paralysed, as he pulled the remnants of the blouse off and tossed it aside.

'Well, looky here, Brad! You ever see a pair like that? Poke your eye out if you weren't careful!'

'Get – get away from me!' Alex cried as she covered her breasts with her hands, kicking Wallis low in the stomach.

He bent over, gasping and as she tried to roll off the table, he hit her across the side of the face. It was a terrible blow for her to take: she had never been beaten in her life before this moment. Her brain seemed to jar loose. Her vision blurred, flared red, then black, then images seemed to break apart and only gradually came back together.

Wallis dragged her upright, slapped her open-handed across the face.

'Stop! Stop it!' she cried. 'I – I don't know where they – went! I swear it!'

Steed motioned for Wallis to hold off hitting her again. He stood in front of the now sobbing girl, put a strong finger beneath her jaw and tilted her face up.

'They must've said something. Just a hint, my dear. Anything at all will be welcome.' Then he leaned closer and added, 'If you don't tell us what we want to know, we'll really start hurting you. Then I'll send Wallis to the hotel to bring your aunt along, and we'll see how long you can hold out while the poor old widow tries to deal with Mr Wallis – who, I might add, does not always act like a gentleman. Would you like to think things over?'

Alex was near collapse: nothing like this had ever happened to her before. She was afraid they would rape her and probably kill her afterwards. . . .

'Please leave my aunt out of this. She's fairly new to widowhood and has nothing to do with this. She just stopped to change stages for Denver.'

'Forget the old bag for the moment,' growled Wallis. 'Just remember she's there within reach if we have to use her. Now, *think* and tell us what we want to know, damn you!' He fumbled at the back pocket of his trousers and as he brought something around said with a vicious grin: 'These might help you make up your mind.' He brandished a small pair of pliers. 'See, what you do is work the points just under a finger nail, clamp down then – pull – and twist and lift.' He gave an exaggerated shudder. 'Ooooh! That awful sound as the nail tears away; almost makes me lose my appetite – almost.'

Alex was on the point of fainting. Her stomach

churned, her legs were jelly. Her breathing was hard but coming in short gasps, as if her lungs weren't getting enough air. She jumped when Wallis opened and closed the well-oiled pliers a few times.

'Look. Best thing is to show you instead of talkin' about it.' He reached for her hand and she cried out, backed away, hands clasped behind her back, eyes so wide they looked as if they would pop from their sockets. She shook her head desperately.

'Please!'

She thought frantically about her conversation with Jarret and Pinney.

'They – never said where they were – going! *No!* Please wait! But I gave them a couple of woollen shirts and mentioned they might be too warm for them. One of them, Mr Rankin, I think, said they would be just right as they were going above the snowline—'

'*Where?*' Steed demanded. 'What damn snowline?'

'I – I don't knows. Mountains and deer were mentioned later but – no – names. That's all I can tell you. Please leave me alone!'

She was sobbing now; Wallis looked disappointed but he didn't put the pliers away, he continued to play with them, opening and closing, opening and closing. He had Alex's full attention.

'You lived here long?' Steed's quiet question caught her off guard and she tore her eyes away from those awful pliers.

'About five . . . almost six years now.'

'Then you must know something of the country. Which mountain ranges have snowcapped peaks all year round?'

'I – I – I'm not sure. There's one range you can see from the river bend. A long distance away, but they have one or two peaks still with snow on them, even in midsummer. They're very high and steep.'

'Which range?' snapped Wallis, raising a threatening hand – *click-click* – smiling crookedly as she cowered. 'Well?'

'They refer to them as the Dreary Mountains, but I don't know if that's the real name.'

Steed arched his eyebrows at Wallis, who nodded slightly; he had heard of the 'Drearies'. Then Wallis smacked her across the face and she lay on her side, trying to control her sobs. He looked at Steed.

'We got time to. . . ?' He gestured to Alex, one of her legs, bare to the thigh, showing through her torn skirt.

Steed looked at her, then shook his head regretfully. 'No. We'd better get this job done. The group's looking for results pronto and if we don't deliver, they'll send someone after *us*.'

'Hell! There's no one better they can send!'

'But plenty almost as good. And they can buy more whenever they want.'

Wallis sneered, looked once more at Alex and put away the pliers. She almost fainted with relief. Then both men left, Wallis turning before closing the door after him:

'Don't set the law on us, sweetie. Or we'll kill him, then come back and burn this dump down around your ears – after I give you a manicure. And that's a promise.'

*

They found Luke Handy in the saloon bar and invited him up to their room.

Handy looked startled, and Steed said in a friendly voice: 'We were rather irritable when we arrived, Luke. That was an abominable stagecoach ride. We were a bit rough on you and we'd like to make it up to you.'

Handy looked from one to the other. His only response was a 'Huh?'

Steed remained calm and said, 'Mr Wallis is just about to purchase a bottle of legally bonded bourbon. Thought we might have a few friendly drinks over a good cigar and . . . so on?'

'Yeah! Sure. Sure thing!' Handy was all for that: free drinks of genuine bourbon; hell, he'd walk from here to El Paso for them.

Up in their room, Wallis opened the balcony door, glanced out and over the edge into the dark, cluttered alley beneath, then turned his head and looked at Steed, eyebrows arched quizzically.

Steed shook his head slightly. 'Close the door, I think, Nash. We won't need it open. I can't abide draughts.'

'Thought we might down a glass or two out here.'

Steed shook his head more definitely. 'Not now.' He had changed his mind about killing Handy who helped himself to his third glass of bourbon. 'Sure hits the spot.'

Wallis slowly closed the door, walked across and yanked the bottle out of Handy's grip. Luke looked up. '*Hey*!'

Steed intervened as Wallis started to bristle.

'Just go easy for a moment, Luke. You're a man who knows this country pretty well, aren't you?'

'I should smile I do!' Handy lowered his voice conspiratorily as he added, 'Outrun the law a couple times, an' once, even a whole damn posse couldn't find me!' He looked proud at the memory and nodded for emphasis. 'That's the damn, stinkin' truth, fellers.'

'Well, that's what we wanted to hear, Luke. Mr Wallis and I want to go north to the mountains known as "the Drearies". We're from California, you see, and don't know this part of the country well at all.'

Handy lifted a finger and touched it lightly to his right eyebrow. 'No trouble. I can take you there blindfolded! That's right in my bailiwick, gents.' He lowered his voice. 'Know some fellers who live around there. They kinda make their own law, you know what I mean? You need extra help, I can get 'em if the pay's right.'

'I think you'll be enough, Luke, old man,' Steed said tightly, while Wallis scowled; both hated having to depend on the likes of Luke Handy. 'And you'll find us generous.'

'Uh-ha! Which reminds me. That re-ward for trackin' down Ben Dodge—'

'We'll double it if you get us to these mountains – er – pronto! Is that what you say out here?'

'Double! Hey, Mr Steed, I'm your man. We'll leave right after sunup.'

Steed shook his head. 'Tonight, Luke. This is an emergency.'

'Oh! Yeah, well, OK. Gimme another shot or two of that bourbon and we'll leave within the hour.' He paused and winked. 'Gonna need lotsa supplies, though, goin' in there; we'll have to pick 'em up first, and a mule to carry 'em. You pay for that, OK?'

'Yes, yes. Now, drink up and we'll go see if the general store's still open.'

'Hell, leave it to old Luke. They'll open up for me.' He squinted. 'That re-ward money, now. . . ?'

'We'll pay you later, Luke – double, remember?'

Luke's eyes brightened and Wallis murmured so only Steed could hear. 'And you'll pay, too, you son of a bitch, before it's over!'

Alex was totally surprised when her aunt came in. Just as the widow was totally surprised to find her niece bruised and battered, clothes torn, bathing a bleeding lip over a basin in the living section of the premises. She ran swiftly to Charlotte, who embraced her enthusiastically.

'My dear! What on earth's happened! The door was open and I. . . .'

Alex at last gave way to the pain and grief she was so desperately trying to hold in. Between sobs and blowing her nose, wiping her eyes, she told the widow what had happened.

'Well, we must fetch the law immediately! Tell me where the sheriff's office is, Alex, and I'll . . .'

Seated in a chair now, a gown wrapped around her, Alex looked up with her reddened eyes and shook her head.

'We only have a county deputy, Aunt, and he's a long way out of town right now. Anyway, I don't want the law. I want to handle this myself.'

'Don't be a silly girl! Handle it yourself *indeed*!'

'Aunt Charlotte, you don't understand. I – I gave way to my . . . fear. I was afraid of being . . . hurt more than I already was and I – I betrayed those men!'

Charlotte had pushed her veil up long since and now a frown creased her forehead. 'Betrayed? What on earth are you talking about?'

'I – I told Wallis and Steed what – what they wanted to know! *I – gave – in!*'

The widow went to the hob where the coffee pot was heating now and poured two cups, adding milk and sugar. Her old hand trembled slightly as she passed one to her niece. Alex took it without seeming to realize what she was doing. She looked up into the widow's face.

'D'you understand what I'm saying, Aunt?' Her voice was steadier now and her shaking had eased. She sipped the coffee, saying '*Ouch!*' as it stung her split lower lip.

'Yes, my dear, I do,' was Charlotte's answer, surprising the younger woman. 'You have inherited your father's sense of fair play – his "code", I believe is the jargon they use in this part of the country. Never betray a friend, stand by your word at all costs – that sort of thing. It is supposed to set a real man apart from others. Oh, I'm not making fun. Your father was my brother and I saw it developing in him as we grew up. Because *our* father followed the same set of principles.'

92

'Then you understand why I have to try and put it right?'

The older woman's eyes were a little sad but she sighed and nodded slowly. 'Yes, dear, I understand, but I'm not sure that I approve! I mean, here I was, coming to see you because I was afraid I had upset you by moving into a hotel room instead of staying here! Such a trivial thing as opposed to what has happened to you! But you must allow me to at least give you some first aid to those cuts and bruises.' She paused and looked steadily at Alex. 'Before you go.'

Alex went very still, stared back, then smiled, ignoring the split lip that began to bleed again.

'Oh, now I know why you were always my favourite aunt!'

They hugged briefly, Charlotte saying very seriously, 'I take it you know where your friends have gone?'

'Only in general.' Alex didn't sound too confident when she said that.

She knew the way to the Dreary Mountains, and it was wild country, inhabited by wilder men: outlaws, trail bums, the occasional Indian, but. . . . She tilted her head, jaw jutting. 'I think I can find them, Aunt. I only hope I can reach them in time.'

Aunt Charlotte looked at her steadily, slowly smiled as she nodded.

'Yes. There's a lot of your father in you, my dear – a lot.' Her smile widened. 'And I'm very proud to say that.'

She dug into her capacious handbag and brought out a small pearl-handled pistol: a five-shot in .32

calibre, no trigger guard, the trigger itself disappearing into a moulded metal fin until the hammer was cocked.

'You may need this. And believe me it is a lot more lethal than it looks. I can assure you from practical experience.'

Alex's hand was quite steady as she took the weapon.

'Thank you, Aunt Charlotte. I think I know how to use one of these and I certainly will if I run into Wallis and Steed again.' She paused and swallowed, sobering. 'But I hope I don't!'

CHAPTER 8

MUCH TOO LATE

They travelled swiftly for the first few miles and then slowed and entered a series of hogback rises.

Pinney volunteered to climb up the first on foot, resting the mounts, and he was away for about twenty minutes. Jarrett became edgy enough to check the loads in his Winchester three times before standing up, ready to follow his pard.

Pinney met him halfway. 'Can't sleep?' he asked. Jarrett could make out a twinkle in his eye.

'Worryin' that you might fall, you being the clumsy coot you are.'

Pinney laughed and they sat down side by side.

'Nothin' to see back there. Worked my way along the crest until I had the glow from the town in the right place: way back and not much, but no silhouettes of any riders. Reckon we can sleep easy tonight.'

'Good. I need a strong cup of java.'

'We gonna make a good team, Dave. I got the same need . . . and a leetle helper to make it set easy.' He held up a flat, part-empty pint bottle of whiskey. 'You won't recognize the brand, but it's sure gotta kick. Good night's sleep guaranteed.'

'We'll need it once we hit those mountains.'

They kept the fire small in a shallow trench that they had scraped out, and dragged a couple of rocks over to further hide the flames. The coffee was strong, well-laced with the whiskey. It hit the spot and they rolled cigarettes from Dave's tobacco sack, sat with their backs against their saddles, smoking and sipping the hot coffee.

'Cooler here even than in town,' ventured Pinney.

'We'll appreciate these shirts once we hit that snow-line.'

They fell silent, too tired for small talk, listened to the night noises for a spell. Then Pinney asked quietly,

'You don't mind the question, Dave. How come you turned bank robber?' Jarrett didn't answer right away and Pinney, thinking he'd made a mistake in asking, said, 'I mean, what I heard, you only robbed two and they caught you on the third, 'cause you stopped to send some doc to a woman birthin' in the bank you just held up.'

'Well, I watched my sister die as a result of a breech birth. What got me started robbing banks was the branch at Tailend, Texas; they foreclosed on my land because of pressure from one of the bank presidents. His kin wanted my corner to add to their holding which was already big enough for Custer's Last Stand

96

and the Battle of Bull Run.'

'The hell you say! Just plain greed!'

'Yeah. First Frontier National was the bank. We went broke. My wife got ill because of all the worry and died eventually. I got mad, blamed the damn bank and set out to rob every damn branch they had. As you know, it didn't last long. They won in the end: got me seven years in Red Rock pen.'

Pinney smoked down his ciagertte and mashed out the stub against a rock. 'I had a short run as an outlaw too. After I gave up lookin' for Ben Dodge, because I was broke and needed a stake, I figured to get it in a hurry. Picked the wrong stage; s'posed to be only an old-timey guard, but turned out there was some special shipment and I got nailed. My name went down on the Red Rock guest list, too.'

'Till you busted out.'

'Yeah, it worked, but only in a kinda backhanded way. I mean, I should've drowned in that river, but I didn't, and I took that as a sign I was meant to find Ben Dodge and finally get my share of the cold, hard cash.'

'You might yet – if we're lucky in the Drearies.'

'*Mighty* damn lucky!'

Pinney spoke as he yawned and blinked. 'Ha! More tired than I figured. You want supper?'

'No, I can hold out till breakfast. We might's well turn in now and get an early start tomorrow.'

The idea was a good one.

Only thing was, they didn't count on Luke Handy's local knowledge.

'They'll be watchin' their backtrail, you can bet on that,' Handy told Wallis and Steed as they veered away from the main trail towards the low, blocky dark bulk of a series of hogback rises. 'Them's low hills but we got moonrise an' the glow of the town, way back but still behind us on this trail.'

'Which means we could be seen!' snapped Wallis.'You sure your name ain't *Un*Handy?' But Luke was confident and held up one big hand.

'Now, easy does it, gents. I want that money you promised and I'll work for it. You just gotta trust me a little more.'

Steed showed him the double-action Smith & Wesson. 'I can get off three shots to your one. That's as much as we'll trust you! Now what're you getting at?'

Handy swallowed and his hand shook a little – though it wasn't noticeable in the dark – as he pointed to the hogbacks. 'Only place between here and the first ranges they can use to see any distance. I'll bet they're camped in there someplace now where they'll be able to see this trail and the surroundin' country come sunup.'

'Well?' snapped Wallis, agreeing but reluctant to let Handy see it.

'They're too smart to show a campfire, but food smells on the night air are just as good as seein' a glow of coals. Ask any Injun.'

Steed and Wallis exchanged barely visible glances

and felt a shade more regard for Luke Handy.

'S'pose they went to bed hungry?' Steed asked.

'Could be. But I'll bet they brewed some java.' He tapped his swollen nose. 'Never knowed any cowpoke who went to bed without his coffee, even if his belly was empty.'

'That nose doesn't look in any condition to pick up such smells,' Wallis observed.

'Well, thanks to that sonuver Dodge – or whatever his real name is – it ain't in top condition. But I bet I can find their camp if they did brew coffee.'

'Well, I'll encourage you some, Luke,' Steed said. 'Fifty dollars in your hand when you lead us into their camp. Quietly.'

'You said the right words, Mr Steed! Just dismount and if one of you'll lead my old jughead, I'll scout ahead and take you right to 'em.'

'Bit free with the money, aren't you?' Wallis said to Steed as Handy slipped away into the darkness.

'Hell, it's not our money. The Group can afford it. They'll pay plenty to get that strongbox back. They already pay us plenty, but maybe we can milk them for just a little bit extra.'

Wallis nodded, but he was leery, too; he knew how damn ruthless the Group could be: human life meant less than a dollop of dung on their shiny, genuine deerhide boots.

Twenty minutes later Handy appeared, grinning. 'Follow me, gents. I believe things are about to get mighty interestin'!'

*

Alex Birdwood had to admit that she had been too ambitious in starting out tonight after her ordeal.

She had lived all her life on the edge of the frontier, mostly in towns but once, for three years, on her father's ranch, before floods wiped him out and ruined him financially and healthwise. She had liked the outdoors, found inspiration in nature, both animals and plants, for her emroidery designs, the colours of the famed Western sunsets, even the swirling shapes of dust storms that occasionally rampaged through the Panhandle where she lived during those years.

But she had never really been what they called a 'ranch woman'. She could ride and rope tolerably well, shoot a rifle, but wasn't exactly a markswoman, and she could cook from a chuckwagon's primitive pantry stock, even do some butchering, but she didn't see herself really as the hardened type of pioneer woman. She had had good, kind parents, was an only child, and had led a mostly sheltered life.

Certainly she had never been manhandled, or beaten and threatened the way she had with Wallis and Steed. Just thinking about it brought a shiver and she felt her fingers curl involuntarily as she remembered those pliers in Wallis's eager hands.

But she did have a strong sense of what was right and what was wrong, and she knew she had done wrong to betray Dave Jarrett and Pat Pinney just to save herself some more hurt. It was a terrible hurt to consider, but she could have lied, even though lying was against her nature, but under the circumstances. . . .

'Oh, stop it, you little fool!' she said aloud, startling her roan mare as she led it into the shadow of some low hills. 'You did what you had to do – and you're *still* trying to salve your conscience. And the only way you can do that is to warn Jarrett and Pinney – if it's not already too late.'

And as the thought came into her head, she stiffened and put the back of a hand against her mouth.

From somewhere ahead and above, came the crash of gunfire.

She was too late after all – much too late.

CHAPTER 9

PAY THE PRICE

It was Jarrett who heard them coming. That second cup of coffee had filled his bladder to stretching point and he had to roll out of his blankets and make for the rounded rock about ten feet from the sleeping area, which they had designated as the Place.

He had finished and was adjusting his trousers when he heard an unmistakable sound, not too loud, but only a boot slipping on loose gravel made such a distinctive scraping, followed by a brief gouging, the trickle of loosened stones, and the thud of a sprawling body.

He was in stockinged feet and tippy-toed back to his bedroll, where he sat down and swiftly pulled on his boots, then reached for his rifle. He poked Pinney in the ribs with it and the man sat up with a jerk and a bewildered. 'Huh?'

Dave grabbed Pat's upper arm and pointed with the

rifle barrel.

'Someone on the slope,' he told him hoarsely.

At the same time a rough voice called: 'Stay put! We got you covered!' Hell! Closer than he thought!

'Cover this!' Dave yelled, diving for the ground and shooting the rifle in two quickly levered shots. He rolled away from Pinney who had scooped up his six-gun, stayed on one knee, and chopped at the hammer. Pat fanned four crashing shots, uncaring about accuracy right now, simply making noise and letting the intruders know this wasn't going to be any walk-over.

Both men were down flat now, Jarrett firing deliberate shots at any movement he thought he saw on the slope below. No one was yelling but there were plenty of curses as the intruders slipped in their hurried efforts to find cover.

He saw a group of stars suddenly blur; he triggered instantly. Someone cried out and they heard the crash of a body, the slipping, sliding sounds as it rolled a few yards downslope.

But someone had homed in on his muzzle flash. He jerked, hands tingling as a lucky bullet struck the rifle barrel and tore it from his grip. He shook his hands vigorously in an effort to get circulation and feeling back into his fingers, fumbling at his six-gun.

Pinney dived sideways, rolled on to his knees and emptied his Colt. He had tried to reach the edge of his blankets so he could snatch up his rifle, but he had slipped on the loose scree and was at least a yard past his bedroll. With a grunt of effort he launched himself back, reaching for the dull gleam of the Winchester.

A boot heel slammed down across his wrist and wrenched a mighty, pain-filled curse from him. Then Wallis slammed his smoking revolver in a backhanded blow, knocked Pinney's hat off as the metal struck his head and stretched him out on the ground, knocked cold.

Jarrett had his own six-gun now but the pressure of a hot ring of steel against the side of his neck made him open his fingers and let it drop. He raised his hands slowly and Steed laughed briefly behind him.

'Nice going, Dodge! But you can't dodge us, eh, Nash?'

Wallace grunted looking about in the dark. 'Where's Handy?'

'Think he got shot.' Steed sounded uncaring: as far as he was concerned Luke Handy had done his job and was of no further interest to him.

Wallis started down the slope, tripped over something and swore. He groped by his leg and jumped: he had found Handy. 'Christ! Blood all over him. Feels like a headshot. Probably die unless he gets to a doctor.'

'I won't even bother to answer that.' Steed suddenly hit Jarrett across the side of the head with his gun and drove him to his knees. Dazed, Dave lifted his hands to his throbbing skull, the night spinning with swirling stars.

'You've given us a long chase, you son of a bitch. But we've got you now and it's time you paid the piper.' Steed leaned towards the semi-conscious man. 'I guess you think you won't tell us just where you've stashed that seventy thousand in cash, but, I promise

104

you, you *will* tell us and be very damn glad to do so. Nash and I have had a lot of experience at this kind of thing. So, just take a short sleep on it like your friend, and we'll get properly started in the morning. Pleasant dreams!'

He didn't give Jarrett time to speak, but gun-whipped him again and Dave plunged into a roaring vortex that dragged him down painfully and swiftly into total blackness.

Alex Birdwood's heart pounded as she heard the horses coming down the slope through the deep darkness of the hollow between the hogbacks.

She reined the roan swiftly into some bushes growing amongst a clump of big rocks and leaned forward in the saddle, stroking the animal's taut neck, calming it, feeling the ears rigid but turning to pick up the sounds of the other riders.

The mare started to whinny but Alex clamped her hand over the quivering lips and nostrils and the motion was enough for the horse to know not to make the sound. It gave a subdued snort and shook its head by way of protest, but remained quiet otherwise.

Mouth dry, Alex stayed crouched over the roan's head and strained to see in the direction the sounds were coming from. It was hard to make out but she had enough night vision to see two riders: Wallis and Steed, she was sure, leading a horse each.

Two bodies were draped over the saddles and she sucked in a sharp breath. *Oh, my God! They've killed them both!*

Then as the riders passed within a few yards, just visible against a large pale rock, she saw rope ends trailing under the bellies of the led mounts. She released her breath slowly, afraid she might be heard, they seemed that close.

Surely they wouldn't bother tying dead men over the saddles, she told herself, not quite convincingly. Wouldn't they just drape them across?

She had to hope so! In which case, Jarrett and Pinney might still be alive – but in what condition?

More important, what could she do about it?

Up the slope near the top of the hogback rise there was movement.

Luke Handy had dragged himself in against a rock, managed to pull himself up to a sitting position, then sank back against the coarse surface. He put a shaky hand to his head, feeling one entire side of his face sticky with a flood of his blood. His right eye was sticky with it as it congealed, blurring his vision. He wiped at it irritably.

That damn Jarrett had almost finished him! The shot had gone just a little high – *thank God!* – ripped a shallow gouge across his scalp and above his ear. It bled like a stuck pig, so copiously that it had actually saved him from Wallis finishing him off; apparently the killer thought Luke was as good as dead anyway and saved a bullet.

Well, he'd have his reckoning with those two. Wallis and Steed: sounded like a stage act, or a firm of lawyers, but it would be more appropriate for a firm of undertakers! And he would see to it that they were their own first customers. He chuckled, a little off-key with shock and the pain in his head; he was feeling the effects of that scalp crease worse than he had allowed.

Leave me to die, would they? I done what they wanted and that's how they were gonna pay me off! Let the coyotes and crows feast on me! 'You bastards!'

He cursed out loud but immediately grabbed at his head, pressing his neckerchief against the throbbing wound. Man, his head was *pounding*! Worse than the worst hangover he could recall; even after that fight with Jarrett it hadn't been this bad.

He closed his eyes and after a minute or two suddenly snapped them open and sat up straighter, immediately regretting the jarring stabbing pain it caused. He let things settle, frowning and squinting into the dark. *It had suddenly come back to him!*

While he had been half-conscious, bleeding, and, he thought, dying, he had heard Steed telling Wallis to leave him on the slope, but Steed had mentioned something else that was important! Yeah, something *damned* important. . . !

'I've got it!'

The words came with an effort, half-strangled, but he didn't care. He started to laugh but that hurt too much, though he didn't care about that either, really. He felt kind of – reckless, because the *important* thing was what Steed had said, apparently talking to Jarrett, just before he gunwhipped him unconscious.

I guess you figure you won't tell us where you've hidden that seventy thousand in cash. . . .

That's what Steed had said: *seventy thousand in cold, hard cash*!

Well, now he knew why Wallis and Steed wanted Jarrett or Ben Dodge or whoever the hell he really was, so damn badly! He had stolen 70,000 bucks from them – and hidden it! And Dodge/Jarrett must be the only one who knew where!

Seventy thousand bucks!

Now that was way too much for one man – and those two gunslingers would soon make Jarrett talk, tell where he had stashed all that dinero – then he could follow and. . . .

All he had to do was lie doggo long enough to get his wits back – and then – well, then he'd see.

He knew, deep down, that he wasn't tough enough to tackle Wallis and Steed by himself, but then he knew these hills pretty damn good and knew the restless, lawless men who inhabited the dark draws, the high peaks and the dry gulches, like Waco Hutch and his wild bunch.

Hell, they'd tear down a whole damn mountain with their bare hands to get even a whiff of that $70,000.

Groggy, sick to his stomach, he started to crawl away, hoping his horse was still down in that dry gulch where he'd left it while he scouted ahead.

It was there.

He sat gasping against a rock, his mount contentedly munching at a patch of grass. He felt like hell; it was going to be a major effort getting up into the saddle.

And then he had to ride away from Steed's camp without noise; if they heard him, he wouldn't make more than a few yards, and Waco Hutch was a lot further away than that.

Still, it was close to a miracle just what a wounded man could do when he had the incentive of $70,000 driving him on.

The dark world reeled about him, the stars seeming to blur in huge wavering circles, the moon dancing a jig over the mountain ranges.

But he was in the saddle now, wrapping the reins about his gravel-scarred hands, starting his mount forward.

He was on his way to being rich.

On – his – way. . . .

If only he could stay in the saddle long enough to reach Waco Hutch and his wild bunch.

On – his – way—

Yee-haar!

But there was no cheering, mentally or otherwise, for Dave Jarrett and Pat Pinney.

They had been handled mighty roughly; when they had arrived back at Steed's and Wallis's campsite Wallis had merely yanked the ropes to release the slip knots and tipped the gunwhipped men off the horses.

Both landed awkwardly and painfully. Pinney gave a half-yell, followed by a brief silence, then cut loose with a stream of swearing such as Jarrett hadn't heard since escaping from the Red Rock penitentiary. It was a picturesque rendition of inventiveness and knowledge of human and animal body parts that left Dave awed.

For himself, he landed hard and had the wind knocked out of him. Any cussing he did was delayed until his senses stopped reeling, and by then Wallis was moving in with lengths of rope or rawhide – and his boots.

He kicked both men in a practised, sadistic pattern, starting at their ankles and working up their legs with particular attention to the shins and knees. Then he moved on to the belly, did some stomping, beat a tattoo on the ribs, found painful nerve spots on the shoulders and outer upper arms and finally – when the victims were writhing and gasping in pain that engulfed their entire bodies – he let them suffer a few minutes, then kicked each man carefully in the temple, sending them spinning into darkness.

Steed wrenched himself around in his blankets and raised up on one elbow.

'Are you finished yet? I want to get some sleep. We can go to work on them properly in the morning.'

Wallis, breathing hard from his exertions, moved over the bleeding, unconscious men to make sure the bonds were tight and cutting into the flesh, then straightened with a small grunt.

'When they come round they'll know what they can look forward to. Only that's just a sample. I'm tired now or I'd refine it a little with the help of a burning cheroot, or my old friend, the pliers. Yeah, maybe I'll pull a couple toenails before I turn in.'

'You damn well won't! They'll scream half the night and *I – want my sleep!* Now, if they're bound tightly get into your bedroll.'

Wallis made sounds of disappointment, gave each man one last kick and headed for his bedroll.

'Mebbe I should gag 'em—'

'Oh, for Chris'sakes, *leave them be and turn in*!'

'Yeah, yeah, all right. Damn spoilsport.'

Lying full length in the darkness above the camp, on the hard ground at the edge of a small arroyo, Alex Birdwood, bit into the soft edge of her hand to keep from crying out.

She felt as if she would be physically sick.

And she couldn't even see what was really happening to Jarrett and Pinney. Could just hear the awful sounds, and her imagination. . . .

How on earth was she going to battle two sadists like those below who could so easily fall asleep after inflicting injuries in such a cold-blooded manner on two helpless men?

She crawled backwards and dropped down off the rim into the small arroyo where the roan mare waited patiently. All she had as a weapon was the five-shot handbag gun that Aunt Charlotte had given her.

Some said it was only good for killing flies, and even then you had to hit them with the butt several times before you were successful.

She was afraid, sick to her core, but she was determined to help these men. It still came down to her having betrayed Jarrett and Pinney, and, no matter what, she saw it as her bounden duty to do all she could.

Even – even if she risked her own life doing it!

And she didn't even realize just how much of a true frontier woman this made her.

CHAPTER 10

AFTER MIDNIGHT

She had no real way of knowing the time; she had never been able to use the stars, though sometimes she had come close to the right hour by judging the sun's angle, but she reckoned she would wait till after midnight.

Just the phrase seemed to conjure up some of the fantastic dime-novel stories of the frontier that appeared on the newsstands occasionally. *After midnight: a witching hour!* But whether the drama was overdone or not, in her mind she decided that Steed and Wallis ought to be asleep by midnight, therefore she wouldn't go in until an hour after.

She had a sharp knife with her, a piece of stag's horn with a four-inch blade set in it. An uncle had given it to her '*For skinnin' jackrabbits, in case your ladies' shop don't take off. No need for you to ever go hungry. . . .*'

But she would if her hunger could only be

appeased by her somehow acquiring a jackrabbit that needed skinning and gutting.

She gave a small shudder at the thought. Well, the blade had never been used by her for that or a similar purpose, but it was razor-sharp and she hoped it would quickly sever Jarrett's and Pinney's bonds.

She had a pair of moccasins in her saddle-bag which she always carried with her; riding boots made her ankles ache if she wore them too long. She put the buckskin shoes on now with their double sole, made specially for her by a half-breed Kiowa in return for a shirt with a red front, a black back, one yellow sleeve and one bright blue. He had been very pleased with the startling result – as she was pleased with the moccasins.

Her heart beat and hammered against her ribs as she tugged down the cuffs of her corduroy trousers after tying the moccasins and stood up, feeling for the knife in its beaded sheath on her belt. Instead of wearing her narrow-brimmed hat she simply tied up her ample black hair with a strip of rawhide, tucked in her shirt more firmly at the waist and – now she could delay no longer. It was time!

So dry was her tongue that it briefly stuck to the roof of her mouth. Alex licked her lips, crouched lower behind her bush and held her breath.

She was listening for the breathing of Steed and Wallis; apparently the prisoners were suffering even in their sleep, such as it was, for there were odd grunts and groans, once a coughing fit as aches and pains no doubt rampaged through their ill-treated bodies.

She stayed put, breathing very shallowly, straining to hear the others. Yes! That was definitely Steed, closer to her than Wallis, who was slightly upslope. She was going to have to make her way around in a semi-circle to get to where the prisoners lay bound. She hoped they were fit enough to make their way down to the small draw where she had discovered that their horses were ground-hitched.

Her biggest fear was that they had suffered more damage from Wallis's sadistic ministrations than she anticipated. She needed them to be able to move mostly under their own steam; she was certainly not strong enough to give them much support, but she would try if necessary.

Surely the pounding of her heart would wake Steed or Wallis! It seemed to be trying to burst through her ribcage and. . . .

She was close to Jarrett now, and she realized he wasn't breathing. *Oh, dear God! Don't let him have succumbed when I'm so close to freeing him!* Then she was startled to hear him ask in a gravelly, hushed voice: 'Who is it?'

She realized that he must have held his breath so as to hear her better, and get a general location.

How he must have been surprised when she answered quietly, 'It's Alex Birdwood – the seamstress.'

Silence. Then, 'I – think I must be dreaming.'

She smiled faintly despite her tension. 'No. I have a knife. I'm feeling for your hands now – ah! Don't move. It's very sharp.'

Three strokes were all it took to sever the rawhide bonds at his hands and feet; she heard the rasp of his clothes as he worked his numbed hands around in front and began to rub them, smothering minute gasps of pain with returning circulation.

'Pinney's up . . . there.' He may have gestured in the direction but she wasn't able to see any movement. 'Be careful. Wallis is pretty close to Pat.'

'Will you and Mr Pinney be able to travel?'

He heard the anxiety in her whispered words and smiled a little, though even that small movement of muscles caused his jaw to ache and pound. His head was thundering and his body throbbed from Wallis's brutal kicking.

'We'll – make it, ma'am.'

She was relieved to hear him say so and then:

'I don't think so, Dodge!'

Alex froze, nearly passing out with the shock of hearing Steed's voice almost in her ear. And then she cried out as steel fingers grabbed her knife hand, twisted the weapon free, tossed it aside, then tightened on her upper arm. She was pulled in against his hard body. He shifted grip so speedily she didn't even realize it until his left forearm clamped across her chest and the hand moved up under her jaw, locked about her throat. At the same time, she felt a gun muzzle in her ribs. She made small, desperate sounds as she struggled futilely.

'Nash! Are you awake?'

There was an unintelligible rumble and them Nash Wallis's sleep-thick voice asked, 'Wha's – matter?'

'Wake up, you damn fool! We have us a wide-eyed, virginal heroine here. She just cut Dodge's bonds and was making her way past you to get to Pinney.'

Wallis was moving long before Steed stopped speaking. He scooped up his six-gun and turned towards Pinney, who lay still and silent, no more than a dark mound, a few feet away. 'I've got him covered, Brad!'

'And I have the girl – plus our friend Dodge. . . .'

'Not yet!'

Jarrett hurled himself at Steed, rammed an elbow against the man's neck. Steed staggered, falling to one knee, dragging the girl down with him. But she fought free and rolled away down the slope as Jarrett kept going, kneeing Steed, snatching at the man's Colt. Steed threw the gun away out of reach but Dave hooked him on the side of the jaw, hurled himself over his body, going after the sliding pistol.

'*Run!*' he yelled at the girl, somersaulting, feeling his muscles wrench as he stretched wildly trying to reach the gun.

'Get outta the way!' yelled Wallis. 'Goddamnit, Brad. *Move!*'

Wallis fired and the sound of the shot slapped through the night, running around the close-by slopes. He triggered again, then Dave had Steed's gun and he twisted on to his back, still sliding down the slope.

His fingers were tingling, not yet having full circulation, and his thumb slid off the hammer spur without cocking it. But it cocked the second time even as Wallis fired again. He heard the lead's snarl as it ripped through the darkness.

Still sliding, head pointing downwards, Dave grabbed the gun in both hands and got off two shots at Steed. The man twisted and ducked, but he had been moving fast, after the girl, at the time, and his fall threw him closer to her. With a wild yell he forced himself to stretch; he felt his fingertips brush her moccasined heel. He heaved up and jabbed harder. He felt her foot twist aside, then miss its grip on the ground as it hooked the ankle of her other leg.

She fell with a crash and screamed as Steed flung himself on top of her.

Although the half-moon was now coming out from behind a bank of cloud, Dave Jarrett couldn't quite make out what had happened, but Alex's scream sent his blood cold. He contorted his aching body, twisting around, heels digging in as he rolled on to his side. He held the Colt in both hands now. His thumb hooked the hammer spur – and froze in that position.

Steed reared up, pulling the dazed girl with him, holding her in front of his body.

'I can snap her neck as easily as a celery stalk, Dodge! I have no use for her except as a means of making you surrender. So her fate is really up to you. D'you agree? Quickly now! I am not pleased with this episode and I will not hesitate to harm her. Oh, yes, I realize that if I kill her you will kill me. But suppose I simply break an arm? Dislocate a shoulder? Snap that most painful and very, very long-healing collar bone? Show some sense, man!'

'Give her to me, Brad! I'll make her scream loud

enough to be heard in Abilene!'

'No need, I think, Nash. Our friend Dodge has already hesitated too long. Just drop the gun, Dodge. Step away – a little more, if you please. Now kneel down with your fingers locked behind your neck. Do it, or, by God, I will break her shoulder!'

Dave obeyed and in a few strides Wallis stood in front of him and drove a foot into his midriff. Jarrett gagged and fell, knees drawn up, writhing, fighting for air.

'Where's the other son of a bitch!' Wallis snapped, looking around wildly. He saw Pinney's huddled form, still bound, and strode across, in the mood for some more sadism.

'Leave him alone!' shouted Alex breathlessly. 'Oh, you – you damn *coward*! Both of you are cowards! You can only be "brave" with women, or men trussed up helplessly like a Thanksgiving turkey! You – you're filthy specimens and don't belong to the human race.'

Wallis blinked, his face darkening even in that wan light with rising rage. But he paused and tensed when Steed laughed.

'Oh, dear me! This is a true comedy, Nash, old friend! A – true – comedy!'

'You got a twisted brain if you can see anythin' funny in this, Brad, *old friend*!'

'Oh, relax, Nash, relax! We've see-sawed back and forth but we still have Dodge and his pardner – and now we have the girl.' He chuckled again. 'Don't you see the funny side of it? She damn near wet her britches, I imagine, coming here to rescue these two.

119

Instead, now she's not only a prisoner, but the very thing we need.'

Wallis looked at him sharply, strained to see. 'You – mean – we can. . . ?'

'Oh, for Chris'sakes, get your mind above your navel! What I mean is that we have her *and* Dodge. How much easier d'you think it will be for us to find out where he stashed the money now? Don't hurry. Give your brain a chance to figure it out and then. . . .'

Wallis smiled, not a nice smile, either.

'Uh-*huh*!' Wallis stepped across to where Dave was slowly getting to his feet. Jarrett tensed, forcing himself to straighten, his guard lifting.

Nash Wallis laughed, a real guffaw, shaking his head and even wagging a finger. 'Nah, nah. You can relax for the moment, Dodge. I ain't gonna work *you* over – well, I might later, just to keep my hand in, but what I mean is, we don't have to work on you right now. Do we?'

He looked directly at the dishevelled girl and Dave froze, his belly knotting. 'Leave her be. She knows nothing about any of this.'

'Hell, that don't matter. She don't have to. See, Brad there went through a list of things he could do to her and it was enough to bring you into line. Now, *me* – well, I got a whole different list of things *I* can do, and, like old Brad said, I do a lot of thinking below my navel – and any good-lookin' gal who happens to be within reach. Like her!'

Wallis flung out his left arm and grabbed the startled, white-faced Alex by the forearm. He yanked her

120

in close and she stumbled, instinctively put out her hands for support and clawed at his chest. He curled his arm about her, laughing as he drew her in tightly and tried to kiss her.

It was a losing battle from the start; she tucked her chin in, lowered her head and twisted and turned, then snapped her head up just when he thought she had surrendered.

Blood spurted from Wallis's nose as he staggered back and the girl spun awkwardly, preparing to run. But Steed almost casually thrust out a leg and entangled hers, so that she fell to hands and knees.

'No! Stay there. Don't try to get up, and you, Dodge, stay put!'

The Colt was covering them both and Wallis stared in disbelief at the blood on his hand. He ripped off his neckerchief and held it over his throbbing nostrils, eyes murderous as he stared steadily at the hard-breathing girl.

'You see the situation now, Dodge?' Steed asked. 'Suppose we give you till sunup to think it over? You and Pinney will be bound hand and foot, back to back – and gagged this time.' Smiling he turned to the girl. 'You, my dear, will sleep next to me—'

'Between us!' snarled Wallis, his words muffled by the blood-soaked kerchief.

'Yes, very well. Between us. Bound and gagged, too, with a rope running to each of our belts.' He laughed briefly. 'Hmmm. I think I feel a mighty comfortable – or perhaps "interesting" might be better – yes, an interesting night coming up. What d'you think, Dodge?'

'I think if either of you touch her you can kiss seventy thousand bucks goodbye.'

Wallis curled a lip and started forward, but Steed's out-thrust left arm stopped him.

The girl was obviously startled by Dave's words and strained to see his face. He said quietly, 'No use you going to work on Pinney, either. I'm the only one knows where the strongbox is. Pinney was double-crossed by Ben Dodge, so he has an interest, but I'm still the only one knows where it is.'

'Hell, we can make you talk!' snapped Wallis. 'You think we can't use the gal to loosen your tongue?'

'Right now, she's keeping my tongue tied in a knot. First time you lay a finger on her and that's the last chance you'll get at the money.'

Wallis snorted and started forward, but once again Steed held him back. 'I think our friend here means it, Nash. I believe he'd really clam up no matter what we did.'

'Then he's a dead man!'

'I don't think he'd go that far. He has the stubborn look, though. There's something you said that puzzles me. You said Pinney was double-crossed "by Dodge". Seems a strange thing to say, when your name is "Dodge".'

'But it isn't. My real name is Dave Jarrett. I'm supposed to be dead, but never mind that part. Thing is, I found Ben Dodge's body and when I went through his things, I came across that army discharge. I figured it was a perfect identification to have and as Dodge was already dead I could get by, using his name.'

Wallis started to interrupt but Steed, his frown barely visible, said, 'Where was this you found Dodge's body?' Jarrett laughed briefly and Steed continued: 'It wouldn't have been on Dreary Mountain, would it? Above the snowline?'

'Well, if it was, I'm the only one of this group who's been there, and it's a big mountain, with lots of snow on the two peaks. Want to guess which is the right one? You'd only have to move a couple thousand tons to find out.'

'So you took Ben Dodge's name, and didn't know his background: army captain, payroll robber. . . .' Steed's voice took on a cunning edge. 'So how would you know about the strongbox?'

'He had it with him,' Dave lied and Steed snapped, 'On his horse?'

'Not the one that threw him and killed him,' Dave said carefully.

Steed was silent for a short time. 'I'm not sure about this. You could be telling the truth.'

'I am. You leave the girl be, and Pinney and me, too, and I'll take you there and show you where I buried Dodge – and his strongbox.'

Steed looked suddenly alert. 'Why did you bury it? Didn't you try to open it?'

'Sure. Had no tools with me and it's iron-bound, plus a padlock as big as my fist.'

Wallis smiled crookedly. 'Aimed to go back for it, din' you?'

'I – might've given it some thought. If we've got a deal, I'll take you to it.'

'You'll take us anyway,' growled Wallis. 'You couldn't stand still and see that gal cut up. You ain't that tough.'

'He's tough enough to've survived four years on Red Rock's chain gang – with a weekly beatin' thrown in, by the meanest guard ever swung a hardwood billy,' cut in Pinney. 'You ever heard of Lacy Corliss?'

'Hell, yeah! Man's a legend.'

'Not quite the word, Nash – he was "infamous". In fact, back in Washington the newsheets are screaming prison reform and Red Rock was mentioned as an outstanding example of "justice" gone wrong. Your Corliss and his fellow guards even got a mention as being suspected of causing several deaths among the prisoners. They've put Red Rock on notice: that they're closing it down, along with several others at the end of the month.' He looked hard at Jarrett. 'So you were a prisoner in one of the most notorious penitentiaries in the state? Hmmmm. So that explains your resilience to – persuasion.'

Dave said nothing and Wallis glared.

'This true, Jarrett?' he demanded.

Dave hesitated briefly. 'Yeah. Prison sawbones put me in some kinda trance. They thought I was dead and shipped me out to a non-existent niece. I just happened on Dodge's body. But I'm still the only one knows where the money is.'

'And – you'll take us there, in exchange for leaving Miss Birdwood in peace? Is that your deal?' Steed spoke slowly, a hard, probing edge to his words.

'That'll get you your seventy thousand.'

124

'All right. We have a deal: and you'd better make sure you hold up your end of it – or whatever Lacy Corliss did to you will seem like a kitten's kiss, I promise you!'

CHAPTER 11

THE DREARIES

Luke Handy wasn't so confident now that he had actually reached the hole-in-the-wall hideout used by Waco Hutch and his boys. There used to be at least five in the gang, but there were only three in the camp when he rode in – and that included the taciturn redhead who had guard duty and escorted him down from one of the high trails, a rifle no more than six inches from his back.

'Who's this?' growled a man who looked almost as wide as he was tall.

'Hell, Waco, you know me! Luke Handy. We done a little "business" together now and again.'

'Name's familiar.' Waco Hutch squinted through the smoke from the camp-fire. 'Hope you ain't 'spectin' me to say "light 'n' eat" 'cause we're a mite short on rations. Havin' to do our own huntin' to keep our bellies full.'

'Hard times, huh?' Handy tried to sound really interested, although it could be his timing was just right to put his proposition to Waco. 'Well, mebbe I can not only put grub in your bellies, but a slew of gold in your pockets.'

That got their attention and Luke began to feel more confident. He sat down on a rock without being asked and the redhead moved his rifle. But Waco lifted a thick finger.

'What you gonna offer us, Luke? I mean, you brung us crumbs before and it suited us at the time. But now we got a heap of trouble brewin' down Boulder way that could see us headin' straight for Red Rock pen – or a set of three unmarked graves. Mebbe four if you don't give us somethin' really good.'

Handy swallowed, not liking the onus being put on him in this way. 'Judas, Waco! I come to do us all a favour! No need for you treat me like this. *Judas*! I thought we was friends!'

'No friends in this game, Luke, just sidekicks. But I figure you never made this ride in here just to pass the time of day, so for chris'sake say your piece or we'll feed you to the wolves! An' there's a whole pack of 'em right up on yonder ridge, waitin'.'

Right on cue, a wolf bayed, long and waveringly.

Handy's heart was pounding, seeing the hard faces and bleak eyes of Hutch, his brother, Alby, and that damn redhead. He licked his lips quickly. 'OK. This is what I got. . . .'

And he spoke swiftly, tumbling a few words together so that Waco lifted a cautionary finger, made him repeat that part.

Handy was quite breathless by the time he had finished, and his belly knotted when he saw their faces.

'You're loco if you think I'll follow anyone – let alone someone like Steed and Wallis – into the Drearies!' Waco spat. 'Hell almighty, man, there are dry-gulches and twistin' draws in there, not to mention high rocks and ridges, all tangled like an old maid's ball of twine she lets the cat play with! Perfect for ambush!'

Waco Hutch had a deep voice for a man only five feet six and half inches tall (very important that you mention that extra 'half' inch!) but he weighed close to 180 pounds, most of it muscle, solid as a tree.

He was proud of his biceps and triceps and pectorals, wore tight shirts so he could flex them and show off when the cloth ripped; he encouraged saloon girls and anyone else to 'feel' his muscles, then put on his show, eagerly awaiting the applause he knew would be forthcoming. He always had a half-dozen spare shirts stuffed in his saddle-bags to replace the ones that were damaged when he flaunted his muscles.

His head was small, which added to the strangeness of his appearance, perched as it was on those wide shoulders. His eyes were beady, cold and dark, on either side of his large beak of a nose. They were half-slitted now as they stared across the dying camp-fire at Luke Handy.

'You want to risk ridin' into a headshot, Luke, you go right ahead; be my guest.'

'Aw, they're in too much of a hurry to stop and set

up an ambush,' Handy replied, helping himself to another cup of the bitter coffee Waco had handed him when he started to speak. He sipped the steaming liquid cautiously, aware of the intensity of Hutch's stare, and added as casually as he could: 'Did I mention the strongbox they're after has seventy thousand in cold, hard cash in it?'

Hutch straightened, and Luke heard stitching in his shirt-seams pop as he tensed his over-developed muscles. Hutch's rail-lean brother, Alby, and the quiet redhead named Ventress, sucked in sharp breaths.

'You musta forgot that part!' Waco said quietly, through gritted teeth. 'Don't forget anythin' else important! Cash, you say?'

'Mostly gold, I hear,' Handy continued, still acting casual. 'Some notes, which could be traced, I guess. But gold's harder to track down they tell me.'

'I never heard nothin' about seventy thousand in gold or cash bein' stolen!' snapped Waco Hutch. 'And, by hell, I wouldn't miss a thing like that!'

'Dunno the full story behind it,' Luke admitted. 'But it's gospel. Army captain called Ben Dodge went off the rails, robbed a pay wagon he knew about. That's all I know, except Steed and Wallis've been sent to get it back, an' they'll kill anyone stands in their way.'

'Aw, one of them nice easy jobs, huh?' growled Alby with a sneer. He turned to his brother. 'You know these two, Waco? Steed and Wallis?'

'Yeah, I've heard of 'em; killin's their business. From back East someplace. Work for some hard boys that've got a lot of pull high up in the Gov'ment. They say they can get away with murder – literally – because of the backin' they've got.'

'Knew it sounded like an easy chore!' Alby mumbled sullenly.

'No one said it was gonna be easy,' Luke snapped, realizing they weren't taking him seriously enough – or were making out they weren't. 'But seventy thousand! Gotta be worth a bit of extra effort and risk, I reckon.' The redhead grunted and Handy took that for support. 'You want to have second thoughts, Waco?'

'Well, it's a damn big risk!' Waco's face hardened as he looked across the fire. 'That much *dinero* is gonna draw attention like flies to a dungheap. I'd want half for myself; you and the boys can divvy-up what's left.'

'Judas priest! I'm the one been shot in the head! I took all the risks!. Half the loot for you, the rest of us split what's left. That ain't fair! Not by a damn sight!'

He looked at Ventress and Alby, hoping for some support, but neither said anything; he got the terrible feeling that he had made a mistake coming here. They'd take the lot, leave him for dead.

Waco's shirt-seams began to pop again. 'That's my deal, Luke. You don't like it, light out.'

'Like hell!' He turned to Ventress and Alby. 'How far would I get without a bullet in the back!' He snorted, sweating freely now. 'What d'you two fellers say, anyway?'

Handy forgot whatever else he was going to say

when he heard a gun hammer cock and the redhead stepped up behind him, pressed his Colt barrel against his spine.

'Be better we three divvy-up all the seventy thousand,' he said in his clipped tones very close to Luke's ear. 'Who says we need you?'

'I'm with Ventress,' spoke up Alby. 'We dun' need Handy, do we, Waco?'

'Aw, he's not such a bad cuss. Done us some favours. But here's my offer, Luke, just like I already said: half for me, rest for you three – or cut it down to two if you like. Hell, that's real fair, I reckon.'

'Wha – what the hell you mean, "cut it down to two"?'

No one said anything.

Handy swallowed, licked his lips, seeing he was getting nowhere fast. The others weren't going to argue with Hutch, so he figured he wouldn't stand a chance. They were taking over! Leaving him out in the cold – the deathly cold! He sighed, gestured wide with his hands.

'Well, I guess that's it, eh?' He laughed bitterly. 'I go along or I'm out all the way!' He cleared his throat, breathing harder now. 'But, maybe I got an ace in the hole.' He looked around at them with a confident tilt to his bandaged head. 'I oughta get extra for bringin' you the deal.'

'Mmmm – he's got somethin' there, boys,' Waco said, lighting a cheroot from a glowing twig. He puffed and his deadly gaze bored through the smoke. 'How about you get your life, Luke? That's a pretty good bonus, ain't it?'

Luke Handy, frowned, hesitated, flicked his gaze around at the three rock-hard faces, nodded briefly. Damn! He'd been a fool to tell them so much – but it was done now. When he spoke again he couldn't keep the note of desperation out of his voice.

'Yeah, OK, OK! I guess I'll go along with your original deal. I ain't happy but it's better'n nothin'. And we better get goin'. See, we don't really need to *follow* 'em. We know they're goin' to the Drearies, and there's only two peaks with snow on 'em to pick from, so I figure we just take that short cut you once told me you know of, Waco, get ahead and wait for 'em to show up. Then see where they go. With any luck, they oughta lead us right to the cash.'

There was a brief silence, then Waco laughed.

'You always did run off at the mouth, Luke. You realize what you've just told us? Hell, we don't need you at all!' He let that sink in to the liberally sweating Handy and said, quietly: 'Ven!'

There was a slight pause, followed by the muffled sound of Ventress's Colt firing as the hammer fell with the barrel pushed hard against Luke Handy's spine.

The other group of gold hunters rode all night, each one dozing in the saddle from time to time. Alex awoke with a start when she found herself leaning dangerously to one side, and Steed reached out and pushed her upright. She was flustered and babbled some sort of thank you, resolved to stay awake from now on.

132

But it was a long, difficult ride through the foothills, and when pale daylight first showed the snowcapped peaks were still a few miles away.

'Made pretty good time, though, considering,' announced Steed, obviously satisfied. He glanced around to where Jarrett and Pinney slumped in their saddles, wrists rubbed raw from their bonds. 'Soon be having to call on your expertise, Dodge. I trust you're ready and that your memory is sharp and clear?'

Dave raised his bruised face, caked with dirt and dried blood. 'The name's Jarrett, and I can only do my best.'

'Oh-ho! Now you have a surprise coming, my friend. *Your* best may not match up with what I consider to be your best. There may be some . . . conflict, but, I assure you, you will be surprised, *astounded,* at how good your memory can become with certain . . . stimulation.'

Dave said nothing, but he could tell that Steed was growing excited now. This kind of thing was the killer's raw meats; he had a growing appetite for it and Dave knew that whatever he did from now on would not be 'satisfactory' as far as Steed was concerned.

He flicked his gaze to where Alex slumped listlessly in her saddle, pale, begrimed, but with a certain stubborn lift to her jaw. Scared but holding up damned good!

He knew she would be the one Steed would use to persuade him.

The truth was, he had very little to tell them now. He had lied, to buy a little time with the night ride, but it was running out and pay-up was fast approaching.

Inevitably, there would be blood spilled.

As they came out of a line of trees the grey, bare foothills of the Dreary Range rose up before them. It was obvious they were going to have to ride up and over the nearest slopes before they reached the base of the first big mountain. It was capped with snow; an edge of a similar snowcap on the next peak rose up beyond it.

Jarrett turned to Steed. 'Be a whole damn lot easier if you cut our hands free for ridin' up those slopes, Steed. Gonna be a lot of zigzagging and I can't control my mount all the time with my knees.'

Steed stared steadily. Wallis just spat and laughed derisively. But Steed surprised Dave and Pinney and Alex by agreeing.

'All right. It sounds reasonable.' He lifted his Smith & Wesson from his cross-draw holster, smiling tightly, indicating the weapon. 'Half-brother to a Gatling gun when you know how to shoot it, Jarrett – and with my special loads! Remember that.'

'And I'll have a Winchester to back it up if we need it,' cut in Wallis.

'Where the hell you think I can go?' Dave asked tautly, holding up his bound wrists. 'No cover on these hills. They look like the left-overs from a Kiowa scalpin' party, they're so damn bare.'

Wallis's knife slashed the rawhide and he looked coldly into Jarrett's face. 'You're on borrowed time, *amigo*.'

'One of us is.'

Wallis's smile tightened and he backhanded Dave, rocking him in the saddle. 'Brad? How about the others?'

'All right. We'll lose too much time if we have to stop and wait for the girl or Pinney, or go back and help 'em loose.'

Wallis seemed uncertain, but when Steed nodded again and blandished his double action Smoth & Wesson pistol he walked his horse over to the girl and cut her bonds before swinging to Pinney and slashing his.

All three rubbed vigorously at their deeply marked wrists, the returning circulation tingling and burning. Steed squinted into the now burning sun.

'I want to be at the foot of the first mountain by noon.'

'You sure like to push things,' Dave told him tightly. Steed continued to stare in that disconcerting way he had. Dave sighed and lifted the reins. 'Well, we better start now.'

Pinney followed, but swung aside to allow the girl to ride between them. She smiled her thanks briefly.

'We oughta keep the gal near us, Brad!' Wallis complained.

Steed shrugged and raised his voice a little. 'For your information, gents, the target will be the girl if either of you tries anything. First bullet will be a wounding one, and maybe the second. But the third. . . .' He made a tut-tutting sound with his lips, shaking his head slowly.

Pinney glanced at the pale Alex. 'Sorry, Alex.'

She forced a smile, on-off. 'I wouldn't say I was prepared for something like this but – well, I'm not unduly surprised.'

Jarrett's dark stare settled on Steed's face.

'We'll have our reckoning, Steed.'

'Oh yes, of that I'm sure. I'm looking forward to it almost as much as Nash is.'

'Huh! You couldn't be!' Wallis said with a crooked smile. 'But first, let the son of a bitch make me rich, Brad!' Wallis stopped, cleared his throat noisily. 'I mean make *us* rich.'

Steed sobered, frowning a little, his piercing gaze making Wallis stiffen slightly.

Dave wondered just who was going to lay claim to this 70,000 dollars. It could be worth remembering, even if he didn't know where the strongbox was hidden.

For all he knew, it wasn't even within miles of the Dreary Mountains.

Things were going to get mighty interesting when Steed and Wallis realized this.

He hoped he would have figured a way out by that time.

He amended the thought: he'd better have figured a way out by that time.

Or there were going to be three new graves on the snowline.

CHAPTER 12

DEATH ON THE SNOWLINE

Alby had the job of lookout. He was standing with legs spread between two boulders, one of which was smaller than the other, the boot on the higher side resting on a natural step.

He lifted the battered field glasses and swept the country below him, figuring how someone had sure known what he was about when he named this place 'the Drearies'. Alby had never seen such grey, drab country, the brush scrubby and what trees there were were gnarled and crotched at odd angles, throwing weird shadows.

But, with no riders in sight, he figured maybe Steed and Wallis weren't travelling as fast as Waco had figured; he shifted the glasses to the slope above the draw that he had been watching. There was more unimpressive country between the snowline and that draw, twisting trails and animal paths. Even the few birds seemed to be avoiding it, except for a large eagle high above, riding the thermals, with a struggling young racoon in its talons.

This peak with the snowcap was kind of creepy, too. There was no clear demarcation between the snow that still managed to cling to the slopes and the gravelly ground. But, only yards above, the snow had piled up, and, higher still, big boulders and an occasional hardy shrub poked through. Streaks and fanlike places showed how the winds whipped through here, shifting snow, changing patterns. There were even a few huge bare rocks, marble-smooth, protruding in two or three places.

He shivered even though he was wearing two shirts and a torn jumper beneath a thick sheepskin jacket that had seen better days.

That was one trouble with this job: the trio, Waco, Ventress and himself, were not equipped for cold weather. They had worked the flatlands and low hills, where a man needed little more than a denim jerkin most of the year. But this place was like a walk-in icebox that he had seen in the meat works at Abilene; if you weren't careful it would freeze your nuts off.

Hey! He said the word loudly in his mind, had enough discipline not to call out loud, made a quick adjustment to the focus and straightened a little more.

'By God, there they are!'

He couldn't believe it. Lord knew why, because Waco had been mighty sure – cocky even – that they would show up right here, on this very trail, and he had dodged posses back and forth across this country for years. Now Alby had had yet another demonstration that his big brother might have layers of muscle from neck to toe, but from the neck up, he had a *brain*!

He clambered down, dropped on to his horse and spurred away downslope. He didn't have to worry about being seen, not from this angle, and he skidded into the small campsite where Waco and Ventress were lounging, smoking and checking their weapons. He quit the saddle so that he ran the last few yards and propped only a couple of feet in front of Waco.

'So they're comin',' Waco said, seeing, agreeably, the disappointment on his brother's face at not having a chance to break the news himself. 'Usin' that trail to the old draw like I said they would.'

Almost pouting, Alby nodded curtly. 'Yeah – an' there's a woman with 'em.' Alby smiled as he said that: he knew that would be news to Waco. 'Handy never mentioned her.'

The muscle-bound man glanced at the redheaded Ventress, who shrugged. 'Well, if she don't step in the way of a bullet, we'll have someone to help us celebrate.'

Alby smiled wider at that. 'Suits me! Eh, Ven?'

The redhead grunted – whatever that meant.

Waco was standing now, flexing his shoulders, but not enough to break any stitches in his shirt beneath the heavy coat.

'Er, how we gonna do this now they're here – or

139

almost – Waco?' Alby asked.

'Told you right from the start to leave that part to me. Now let's get up far enough so we got the high ground – and *stay hid*! We don't want 'em to see us yet. Let 'em settle in, make their way to wherever the strongbox is, *then* we make our move; and, gents, if the woman's a looker, try not to shoot her – fatally, least-ways.'

They were all smiling now, even Ventress, as they gathered their things; then, rifles resting across their thighs, they rode away from their camp on to the high ground of the peak's lower slopes.

Pinney put his mount in close to Jarrett's as they turned a bend in the trail leading upwards, flicked his eyes briefly towards Steed, who was leading, and said,

'I din' realize there was so much snow! Blinding, too. You sure you can find where you buried Dodge?'

Jarrett swivelled his eyes towards him, hesitated, then shook his head. 'Not sure after all this time. And the lie of the snow's changed with melt and falls. The peak looks . . . different. Can't see anything I tried to remember as a landmark.'

Pinney swore softly. 'Don't say no more! My guts is churnin' already. You said you could find the grave again!'

'Mebbe I can. But it's gonna take time and friend Steed ain't what you'd call a patient man.'

Pinney groaned. 'God help us! And what about Alex? Either of us makes a mistake and he takes it out on her. Which ain't fair, Dave.'

Jarrett nodded. 'It's been on my mind some. Just have to try and convince 'em we're doing all we can and—'

'Watch o—'

Pinney didn't get to finish the warning.

Wallis came spurring in and rammed his mount full tilt into Jarrett's. The horses tangled and squealed and thrashed and Jarrett threw himself out of the saddle, giving his mount a chance to dodge the aggressive horse and get out of its way.

Wallis, mouth twisted, leaned down swinging his rifle by the barrel, aiming the blow at Dave's head. It swept his hat off and the brass buttplate dragged across his scalp, tearing flesh, sending searing pain driving into his skull. Stars burst behind his eyes. His very teeth seemed to jar loose in his gums. His vision blurred and he staggered, fell to one knee. Wallis, triumphant now, started to lift the rifle for another blow.

But, groggy as he was, Dave grabbed the weapon and yanked hard. Wallis cried out as he was pulled from the saddle, hit the ground at Dave's feet, though still clinging to his rifle. Dave kicked him, aiming at his head, missed and took him on the shoulder. The force twisted Wallis and he slid on gravel, groping for his six-gun as Steed's voice suddenly roared, 'Dodge!'

As Dave jerked his head up, Alex screamed and he felt goosebumps sweep over his entire body.

Steed had her hair pulled tight in his left hand, had yanked her head right back so that she was looking skywards, her throat white and straining, hands groping, trying futilely to break the grip. Steed's right hand held the big Smith & Wesson pistol. The muzzle was pressed against the terrified girl's thigh.

'She has very nice legs, this woman,' Steed said flatly. 'Be a shame to have to change the tense so it comes out as "She *had* nice legs – once!" '

Dave released the rifle and Wallis thrust him aside, driving the butt into his midriff. Dave went down, gagging, and Wallis put a knee into his face, the force of the blow knocking him several feet, arms flung out for balance.

He hit hard, spread-eagled and Nash Wallis stepped in, raised the rifle, ready to smash the butt into his face.

'Enough, Nash, for God's sake!' Steed said firmly and tiredly. 'This is the man who knows where the strongbox is, you damn fool! And here you are doing your best to kill him.'

Wallis's eyes were burning with fury. 'Hell, I fix his wagon, we still got Pinney!'

Steed shook his head slowly, bleak gaze boring into Pinney. 'You know where the box is buried, Mr Pinney?'

'No – and that's gospel.'

'But you did help with the robbery?'

'Yeah, yeah. We weren't expectin' all that cash and gold. It kinda sent Ben loco. I know I couldn't take it in at first. Man, it was a *sight*!'

'Never mind the goddam history,' snapped Wallis, still holding his rifle threateningly on the dazed Jarrett. 'What happened after you seen all that cash and gold coins?'

Pinney smiled wryly. 'We figured we could be dead men. Ben guessed it was graft for the congressmen in Washington, said we should hide it for a spell, let things cool down before we tried to spend any of it.'

'Then you were with him when he buried it here!' Steed said flatly.

'No! Hell I never got this far. Ben was thinkin' of his wife, Giselle, see? She run off with a drummer because Ben'd lost his discharge pay and so on; was broke, in other words, and she loved money! Ben, I guess, saw this loot as his chance to get Giselle back. I – just wanted a pocketful of gold coins and some packets of paper money, but he went crazy, threw me off a cliff. I survived but never seen him again till we met up in Boulder.'

Steed frowned, staring from Pinney to Jarrett and back again.

'I wouldn't've thought you'd have been friendly after your experience.' There was suspicion in Steed's words and his looks and in the way he stood.

Pinney glanced at Jarrett who said, 'Might's well tell him, Pat. I tried but he won't believe I'm not Ben Dodge.'

'Jesus Christ!' exploded Wallis. 'Are we back to that again! Brad, all this stallin' is just that: *stallin'*! I'm beginnin' to think they really dunno where the damn money is!'

Steed remained silent a few moments, hard eyes drilling into Jarrett. 'Tell me that isn't so, whatever your name is!' Steed demanded of Jarrett, who shrugged.

'We've come this far. I reckon I can find where I buried the real Dodge.'

Wallis spat a curse and moved in, but Steed held up a hand, face as deadly as a diamondback rattler's that's about to strike.

'I suspect we've been had to some degree, Nash, but there's only one real way to get co-operation – which means the truth.'

Jarrett clenched his fists, looking at the white-faced Alex.

'Leave her be, Steed! She shouldn't even be here! She knows nothing about the strongbox or any part of it!'

'Yes, I reached that decision not so long ago. But she still has her uses just the same.'

'No! I'll do what I can to find the box but leave her—'

'Do what you can?' Steed shouted, face darkening. 'If you think you're going to fob me off with a new pack of lies, then I have something that will bring you to your senses – immediately!'

He spun slightly to the right and shot Pinney where he stood, the high-power load knocking Pat several feet before his legs folded under him and he collapsed, in the snow which was already splashed with crimson.

Breathing hard, more from emotion than any great exertion, Bradford Steed lifted his smoking gun and pointed it at Alex.

'There are spades on the packmule, Mr *Jarrett*!'

144

CHAPTER 13

GRAVE BUSINESS

Steed's face was unreadable as the sound of the shot slapped away through the ranges, dwindling swiftly.

Jarrett's hands clenched into fists and Alex's teeth tugged at her lower lip, her features very white and worried.

Wallis grinned coldly. 'You can bury Pinney when we have time. No one walks away from a hit by one of them bullets.'

'I'd like to make sure,' Dave said tightly and Steed jerked the smoking gun barrel.

'I understand. But one step in his direction will put you right down alongside him.'

Dave let his gaze linger briefly on the unmoving Pinney, then lifted it to where Alex sat her mount some ten yards downslope. She looked very pale and the back of her hand was against her mouth now, a gesture of horror after the cold-blooded shooting of Pat Pinney.

The horror increased when she realized that now

she was the only hostage Steed and Wallis had; they would be just as ruthless with her demise when she had outlived her usefulness, though, remembering Wallis's pliers and shuddering at the thought, they might prolong it.

Just as she decided that now she felt as if she would be able to use her small gun on someone like Steed, there was a yell and a man appeared on the rim of a flat rock that projected out of the snow, to the right and some feet above the digging site.

'Don't go killin' nobody else till you make sure they've dug up the box, Steed, you damn fool!'

It was Waco Hutch. Hard on his words he lifted a shotgun and its thunder smashed across the pristine white slope. Steed dropped flat and, crouching low in her saddle now, Alex saw the buckshot rip up a large area of snow near him.

As it flew up, with gravel from beneath the layer of snow, Wallis threw himself sideways and down, sliding over the snow on his belly, rifle pushed out in front of him. He triggered, a wild shot, diverting the attention of the other two men who rose from either side of Hutch, guns hammering.

'Ride, Alex!' Jarrett yelled, throwing his spade at Wallis. He dived for what cover there was behind the bank of snow where he had been about to start digging.

He heard the splat of lead, saw the girl lift her reins then his face was buried in the freezing snow, crunching against his eyes, nostrils and mouth. He wrenched his head aside, coughing, saw he was sliding past Pinney's still figure, gathering speed.

Steed and Wallis were exchanging lead with Hutch and his men. Ventress had jumped down from the rock and landed waist-deep in snow. But he had kept his arms raised, rifle free, and brought it down and around to his shoulder now. He sighted swiftly and triggered.

Alex cried out as her horse was shot from under her and she flew over the arched neck, her coat flying around her like a pair of dark wings before she hit the slope. She rolled no more than a yard, then her flailing arms and knees dug into the snow, bringing her to a halt. Breathless and amazed to find herself still alive, she lay there, pressing her body into the snow as bullets flew above her, a couple streaking into snow only inches above her burrowing head.

She thought her heart would break through her chest, it was beating so hard and fast.

Alby Hutch saw her go down and even in the midst of the gunfight he began to make his way down towards her, floundering hip-deep, rifle braced and shooting at Steed and Wallis. Ventress and Waco spread out, the latter's shotgun thundering again.

A large block of snow shifted on a steep part of the slope, sliced off like a lump of cheese, dropping in a single solid mass. It landed only feet from Alby, then burst all over him, hundreds of pounds of icy powder and crystals burying him, carrying him down the slope several yards.

His arms flailed and his upper body appeared as he choked and spluttered, still holding his rifle.

Then a body hurtled in front of him. He rocked as the weapon was jerked from his grip ans Jarrett rolled away, sliding on his back. Jarrett brought the rifle around even as he continued to slide, working the lever. Ventress had lost his hat and his red hair stood out against the snow.

His head exploded like a watermelon hit with an axe-handle as Dave's bullet struck home. Dave thought he heard Alex scream but the thunder of the shooting distorted all sound and he wasn't sure.

Then hot lead was boring through the snow, spitting ice crystals into his face as he hurled himself down even further, starting to slide again.

Out of the corner of one eye he caught a movement to his left and above; he snapped his head around and saw Wallis, now on one knee, bringing his rifle to his shoulder. Dave triggered one-handed, the barrel jumped, but the bullet took Wallis in the chest. He went over backwards, tried to bring his rifle up and get off one last shot.

But it was Waco Hutch's lead that tore out Wallis's throat and he crashed sideways, hands clawing at the wound, blood spraying copiously. Hutch had dropped his empty shotgun earlier; now, using his rifle, he beaded Jarrett, then suddenly recognized the man and held his fire as he yelled,

'I got a use for you, Jarrett! Stay put and I'll give you cover.'

'Like hell!'

Steed shouted the words and his Smith & Wesson crashed in a blurred volley of three shots, reminiscent of a Gatling gun raking an enemy line. Waco fell with not much of his head intact. But even as the man was disappearing into the snowbank, the smoking weapon swung towards Jarrett.

'I don't believe keeping you alive is any advantage at this stage either, Jarrett!'

'Don't agree!' Dave yelled. He wrenched free of the snow when he felt his boots touch solid ground, or maybe a rock, leg muscles screaming as they bunched and hurled him clear.

He was still in mid-air when Steed fired, gun in both hands now, finger working the trigger in a blur. But he had put three bullets into Waco and only his sixth – the last – bullet of this volley came close to hitting Jarrett.

It tore at his shirt – the one Alex had given him – seared across his lower ribs and spun his body away from the direction of his original trajectory.

He grunted as the breath slammed out of him and Alex cried out as he tangled with her while she was trying to get behind her downed horse for shelter. He snatched at her, caught a flap of the old coat she was wearing against the mountain cold, and jerked her down beside him. Together they crouched behind the still-warm body of the dead horse.

'Stay down!' Dave gasped unnecessarily.

Steed had reloaded by now, and he put two very fast shots into the horse's carcass. Alex winced and Dave's arm clamped across her shoulders, pushing her down low. He lifted his head slowly until his eyes just cleared the horse's hip. He saw the dead men littering the slope, a few weapons were visible, some half-buried or lying on top of the snow, but gradually sinking.

'Damn! I've got to get to one of those guns and

hope it's still loaded!' He spoke aloud but it was only a thought and he hadn't realized that Alex had heard his words until she tugged his bloody shirt and pulled him down.

Steed emptied the pistol again and was now reloading, when Dave felt metal against his hand. he looked down in surprise at the small revolver that Alex was pressing into his palm.

'Here – it's fully loaded.'

He blinked and stared, first at the weapon, then at the girl. 'What with? Dried peas?'

She frowned. 'No! Of course not. Real bullets. Aunt Charlotte always carries it when she travels. They searched me, but not my saddle-bags. Wallis started to, but I had the gun well wrapped in some fabric with lots of pins and needles stuck in it. He only got pricked twice before he gave up.'

Dave looked at her and smiled. 'You're some kinda special woman. Alex.'

She was embarrassed and he laughed briefly, hefted the almost weightless weapon. This! Against the latest Smith & Wesson, double-action, in .45 express calibre! Bullets that could explode a rainbutt, or knock a constipated grizzly on to his ass!

'It's better than nothing, isn't it?' the girl asked, with a little edge to her words, sensing his lack of gratitude.

'I ain't so sure about that!'

'Well, you know how to shoot it, don't you? Aunt Charlotte showed me and I think I can remember if you—'

He pushed her down, burying her face in the snow

again as Steed raked their shelter. Snow and gravel spat. He laughed, playing with them, so taken with the superiority of his weapon that he couldn't keep from gloating.

'I've plenty of ammunition, Jarrett! Tell you what: you come out with your hands up and continue digging and I'll let the girl live!'

Alex's fingers tightened on his arm at that. He felt a wave of dizziness and knew the wound was beginning to affect him: shock was setting in. So he would have to do something mighty fast in case it got bad enough to incapacitate him. . . .

'Next time he stops to reload,' he said hoarsely, gripping her shoulder, 'just let me take control of you. We're going over the edge.'

'My God! We might be killed. . . .' She let the words fade as she realized that they were in greater danger of being killed if they stayed put. 'I – I – whatever you say!'

Steed's last bullet in that load whined overhead and Dave snapped, '*Now*!'

He dragged her up with him as he rose and, still keeping his grip on her arm, lunged for the edge of the steep slope.

But Steed wasn't the fool Dave had taken him for; sure, he was amusing himself with his fast-shooting gun, but he had the reloaded rifle beside him, too. Now he snatched it up as the two fugitives appeared.

The first was a wild snapshot; Dave and the girl had already started to drop over the edge when he triggered again. He didn't see where his shot went, but he rose up swiftly and levered fast, emptying the rifle's

151

magazine in a frenzy.

'By God! I will *not* let you escape after all this!' he shouted. He snatched up the Smith & Wesson and began taking cartridges from his belt loops, thumbing them home into the big blued cylinder even as he ran downhill. 'I want to see you *dead.*'

'You'll never see the strongbox, then!' yelled Dave.

Steed wasn't prepared for the steep drop past the edge. He felt his stomach lurch as he fell, glimpsing Dave and Alex, hand-in-hand, on their feet now, running round the base of a big sandstone bulge that looked as smooth as an eggshell.

He hit the snow to one side of the huge, exposed rock, and saw how the flatrock overhang projected above, making a deep, snug cavity underneath, giving plenty of protection.

His teeth bared, he worked his legs and free hand to direct his body towards the sandstone. It was muscle-wrenching work and he tried to keep an eye on his quarry below. He was just in time to see Jarrett drag the girl down behind a deadfall, their motion shaking some of the powdered snow loose from the stark branches. He had the breath battered out of him, but he reached out with his left hand and grabbed at the rock.

It was much smoother even than it looked. It had been protected from wind and rain, so there was no erosion to give a handhold. But he twisted and rolled on to it, spread his arms and legs, the greater area of his body slowing his momentum until he stopped, clothes ripped and missing some hide. He lunged into the narrow angle in a wild dive, hurting his left hand

and losing his hat.

But he was safe here, tucked in, right up under the angle of the flatrock where it projected above, meeting the rounded face of the massive sandstone boulder. It must be bigger under the surface than any building Steed had ever seen.

Then there was a small '*pop*', barely audible. He frowned, even as something made a little whistling sound and a short grey sreak appeared across the rock near his feet.

He stared, puzzled, then roared with laughter, looked down to the deadfall and saw a wisp of smoke rising above the bark.

'Oh, my dear Lord!' he bellowed. 'What the hell is that thing you're shooting, Jarrett? D'you think you can bluff me with a kid's toy! Now that's not worthy of you, thinking I would fall for some fool trick like that!'

'That was just a ranging shot, Steed.'

Dave's voice echoed and boomed around Steed way up here so close under the flatrock.

'Ranging shot? You're lucky that that . . . pellet even carried this far! Oh, what a damn fool you've turned out to be!'

Steed lifted the Smith & Wesson and triggered two shots in the space of a heartbeat, their booming slapping at his ears, and still making Alex and Jarrett duck.

Bark erupted from the deadfall, handfuls of splinters thrumming.

'That's what you're up against, Jarrett! You've outlived your usefulness now that the grave's been opened by the snowslide, thanks to Waco Hutch. So if you and the lady wish to prepare youselves in any way for your journey into the Great Unknown, please do so – but quickly! My trigger finger is itching and—'

The rest of his words were drowned out in a series of sharp, brittle cracks, like dry twigs snapping, nowhere near as rapid as shots from Steed's pistol, but very fast considering the somewhat crude weapon Dave was using.

Dave fired his small bullets into the roof, the under-side of the projecting flatrock, only a foot or so above Steed's head.

They ricocheted with a series of small buzzes and whines. Steed suddenly started to laugh, shuddered and reeled, gasping, making terrible gagging, dying sounds as the flattened pieces of lead tore at his head and face and throat.

He lurched forward and began to slide and roll down the smooth face of the sandstone, spinning and cartwheeling before he eventually brought up hard against the deadfall.

The big Smith & Wesson clattered and spun and twisted as it slid off the edge of the huge boulder, then plopped into the snow, the hot barrel hissing briefly.

Alex, pale and shaking, stared wide-eyed at Dave as he held the small, smoking gun, now empty. He smiled.

'You want a souvenir?'

She shuddered and she shook her head quickly, her mouth forming '*No*!' soundlessly.

'Well, bless Aunt Charlotte, anyway.'

*

It was quite a climb to get back to where the shoot-out had started. Searching for a way up round the sandstone bulge, they found the tracks left by Waco Hutch and his men.

Their horses were ground-hitched in a small draw and they both mounted and Dave led the way. But they had to dismount and drag the horses by the reins in the steep parts; Hutch would never have risked riding up to the snowline because this part, though negotiable, was too difficult to be tackled in silence. They would have alerted Steed and Wallis had they used the horses all the way.

But once past the steepest part, Jarrett and Alex could mount once again; ten minutes later the blowing, sweating mounts deposited them at the scene of the shoot-out.

The legs of two dead men stuck out from under a wall of snow, presumably the large block that had been jarred loose by all the gunshots.

Dave recognized Wallis's trousers; the other legs must have been of one of Hutch's men. He was relieved that they didn't belong to Pinney, though he didn't know whether the man was alive or not. He had dropped with that single shot from Steed's double-action revolver and never moved since, as far as Dave knew.

Alex gave a gasp, and when he snapped his head round he saw that she had the back of a hand against her mouth, staring at something.

He followed her gaze and felt himself tense.

The dislodging of the snow had exposed the grave he had made for Ben Dodge; the body was hanging out now, just a few feet above where Pinney lay. The cold had preserved the flesh to some extent but Ben Dodge was not a pretty picture. Dave had never seen the man alive but guessed that, even if he had, he would probably have had trouble recognizing him from the leathery mask of flesh stretched over what must have been a hard-planed face, lips drawn back in a sculpted snarl, teeth gleaming. The eyes were open and staring blankly, though they still had a blue tinge.

It was the stuff of nightmares; he picked up a jacket Pinney had been wearing earlier and draped it over the corpse's head and shoulders.

'We'll move down a little,' he said, taking the girl by the elbow.

Then stopped in mid-step, almost pulling her off balance. He pointed to where Pinney had fallen – the snow now patched red with his blood. The girl gasped, tightened her grip on his arm. Stupid with pain, Pinney had somehow crawled away.

'Where is he?' she asked, looking around quickly. They saw the drag marks in the snow, leading round the rock near where Pinney had fallen.

They started running, slipping, floundering, searching, hoping. . . .

They found him on the far side of the rock, leaning back, holding a wadded kerchief against a terrible wound in his side, low down under the left ribs. Blood ran in a ribbon from his mouth, dripped from his jaw. He looked glazed, not fully aware of his situation. Jarrett knelt quickly, trying to ease the bloody cloth away to see the extent of the wound.

'No!' Pinney gasped. 'Bleedin' bad – Dave . . .' even as he spoke he coughed and blood sprayed. Dave moved back quickly. More blood trickled from a corner of Pinney's mouth.

'I – I'm through, Dave. . . .'

His words were raspy, bubbling in his throat.

'Hell, we can do something, can't we!'

Pinney's head moved from side to side. 'Never reach a doc – in time. . . .'

'We must try!' Alex said. 'I know some first aid. We can pack snow around the wound, for a start. It'll help slow the bleeding.'

Dave looked at her with some admiration. He knew she would try, too – even though she must be repulsed by this kind of thing. She might be what some folk would call a 'greenhorn' but she had guts – would suppress her own feelings and get the job done, worrying about her perceptions afterwards. . . .

The stuff of heroines was the phrase that came into his mind.

He touched her hand and shook his head slowly. 'It's – a very bad wound, Alex. Beyond anything we can do.'

'We must *try*,' she insisted.

'Ma'am, it'd only gimme – more – pain an' – I – I got enough of that. . . .' Pinney rolled his eyes towards Jarrett. 'Dave, I – seen the body before – I crawled off. . . .'

'The snowslide opened the grave right up—'

'It – it ain't Ben – Dodge.'

There was a stunned silence, broken only by

Pinney's hard, wet breathing.

Alex looked bewilderedly at Jarrett, who frowned.

'You sure, Pat? I mean, if that was my brother I wouldn't like to swear to it.'

Pinney coughed more blood. When he had settled he croaked: 'I was his sergeant for seven years. Ben had a bigger – jaw – hair was – lighter – I'm – tellin' you – that ain't Ben Dodge in that grave.'

'Then who the hell. . . ?'

'The – drummer.'

As Dave reared back, puzzled, Pinney almost smiled.

'The one – Giselle ran off with. Looks like – Ben caught up with 'em. I'd say was him broke the feller's neck – not bein' thrown by – his – mount.'

'Then where – where the hell is the strongbox with all that cold, hard cash?'

He began to search near the grave itself, trying to remember at which end he'd buried the box of dynamite, knowing damn well there was no strongbox anywhere near.

But he found the dynamite, and sat back on his hams, staring at it.

After a while, just before he died with a series of blood-spraying coughs, Pat Pinney rallied and said: 'Find Giselle, you'll find Ben. He'll have the – money. But you got the – whole – damn world to search, Dave. Giselle always hankered to – see the big cities: Paris, London 'n' so on. It riled the – hell outta Ben that he – couldn't take her an' show 'em to – her – but now. . . .'

158

Dave nodded slowly as Pinney's voice faded. 'Yeah, now he can.' He saw the glisten of tears in Alex's eyes as he added, 'And I bet that's just what the son of a bitch is doing! We'll never see either of 'em again.'

They rode away from that place of death at mid-afternoon.

Pinney was the only one with anything like a decent grave, even had a crude cross planted on top of the earth mound.

For the others, Jarrett had dragged the bodies into a pile at the foot of a snowdrift, had gingerly opened the box of sweating dynamite, leaving Alex way down the slope and holding the mounts in a draw.

His mouth was dry and his heart hammering as he held the two fused and primed sticks, lit them from a match held in a hand he couldn't quite keep from trembling, then threw them as high up into the snow as he could.

It was a frantic, tumble-and-slide down the mountain and he hurled himself into the draw where the anxious girl waited a split second before the dynamite exploded. The crack was something of a let-down, not the usual ear-splitting roar.

But it was enough to dislodge several hundred tons of snow to cover the dead, maybe for ever.

Just before sundown they paused on the crest of a rise and looked back. The Drearies seemed as uninviting as ever, a faint haze still drifting from the explosion. But sunlight glared back at them from long slopes of pristine white snow, giving no hint of what lay beneath.

'What will you do now?' Alex asked. He took his time answering, looking into her pinched face.

'Well, for a start I'll order four warm shirts from you, seeing as winter is coming.' He smiled as her mouth dropped open: it was the last thing she had expected. 'I'll pick them up when I come back from Red Rock.'

Her teeth clicked together and puzzlement made her frown. 'Why on earth would you want to go back to that dreadful place?' She started to say more, then her gaze sharpened.'Oh!'

He nodded slowly. 'I figure I can make it back there before the end of the month.'

'Of course. When they close down the penitentiary, and when this man Corliss rides out for the last time, you'll be waiting.'

He didn't answer but their gazes held steady.

She nodded gently.

'Yes. You're that kind of man – and with good reason.'

'I'll be back to collect my shirts,' he assured her and her smiled widened just a little.

'They'll be ready and waiting. And so will I.'

'Know something?' he said lifting his reins and ranging alongside her horse as they rode on. 'That sounds a whole lot better to me than seventy thousand dollars in cold, hard cash.'